Save the

DATE

K.S. THOMAS

Save the **DATE** is a work of fiction. All characters and subject matter are the products of the author's imagination. Any resemblance to real persons, alive of dead, is entirely coincidental.

COVER BY SOLOUD!MEDIA
www.soloudmedia.de

EDITING BY WENDY SMITH

Acknowledgements

It's pretty safe to say that I have been seeking out grand stories of love since before I was old enough to know what I was really looking for. A hopeless romantic to the very core with an overactive imagination, I can usually spot them where they don't even exist. As was the case with this one.

So…I would like to start by thanking the little girl with the big brown eyes and the kindhearted boy with his fishing pole. You both set my imagination abuzz and I've had a blast on this journey of what perhaps could have been in another world, another time, another dimension…

On a more practical note, I would like to thank my wonderful Beta Readers. Stephanie and Simone – Thank you for taking time out of your busy lives to help me with yet another project. Your feedback has been invaluable to me.

Same can be said for my editor, Wendy. Thank you!

I would also like to thank David Wuerdemann at SoLoud!Media for creating such a gorgeous cover on a moment's notice! You came through for me in such a huge way and I am beyond grateful. Thank you.

As always, I owe an ocean of gratitude to those I love and am lucky to be loved by ☺

Your support means more to me than you will ever know ♡.

Last, but certainly no least, I would like to thank YOU! Thank you for reading this book. I hope you enjoy Calista and Emerson's journey as much as I have enjoyed writing it.

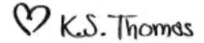 K.S. Thomas

Table Of Contents

Prologue

Until I was six, I was fairly certain I would grow up to marry Prince Eric from The Little Mermaid. Then came the summer we spent at the family lake house and Emerson Barrett. Prince Eric was history.

Before that vacation we spent on Kentucky Lake, I had never met my mother's side of the family. I had heard a great deal of talk though, regarding her childhood growing up on a farm in Lexington. Not that I really knew where that was, but I definitely knew what a farm was, or at least, I thought I knew, even if I hadn't ever seen one, and I was enthralled with the romantic notion of it all. While I never quite understood it, my mother never seemed to share those feelings.

She was the youngest of eight and the only one to spread her wings and fly off to the big city. That's where my childhood was taking place, in Manhattan. There weren't exactly a whole lot of farms to view around my neighborhood. Suffice it to say, I was eager to get my own slice of the Ashcraft Family way of living and I was happy to pick up whatever scraps my mother had thrown by the wayside.

The lake house in and it of itself had seemed majestic to me. Where I was from people didn't live in houses, they lived in buildings. And even though I was accustomed to a rather luxurious standard of living, thanks to both of my extremely successful parents, there simply was no comparing our loft to the eight-thousand square foot log cabin and its wrap-around decks overlooking the lake and the seventy-five acres of lush green that surrounded it.

I was in city kid heaven. Then, once I actually stepped inside, things only got better. An only child, my most constant companions were adults, but here, those were the minority. While I still wound up being the youngest in the bunch, at least I was getting closer to bridging the gap in age between myself and my play mates. I had cousins. Fifteen of them to be exact. All ranging in ages from eight to twenty-three. It was amazing.

Then, there was Emerson. He had tagged along with my cousin Spencer and somehow I had latched onto him two seconds later. Everywhere Spence and Emerson went, there I was, completely oblivious to the fact that two sixteen year old boys probably had better things to do than babysit a grade-schooler. Neither of them ever complained, however. I guess they found me pretty entertaining for the most part, not that I was trying to be.

Most of our days were filled by sitting on the docks with our fishing rods, or hiking through the surrounding woods in search of the local wildlife. At night I would insist on staying up as long as possible, hanging out in the big kids' room drawing pictures while the teenagers told jokes I didn't understand, and played video games.

The summer was nearly over when my mother found me sitting alone in the kitchen one afternoon, busy coloring away in the scrapbook she had given me to fill for the summer. She was always big on things like that. I think it came with her job. She was an upscale wedding planner and was constantly putting together these amazing presentations that looked more like extravagant 3D wedding collages. I wouldn't be surprised one bit, if that was what made brides choose her over all the others. My mother had a way of bringing fairy tales to life. And according to her, every bride was really just another princess looking for her happily ever after.

"What are you doing in here all by yourself, Lissy?" She gently stroked my long brown hair as she walked by.

"Just coloring," I mumbled. I was concentrating heavily on the project at hand. It was serious business and I had no intention of getting distracted.

My mother smiled and went to pour me a glass of milk. "Where are all the other kids?"

"Down by the water watching Geoffrey do tricks on his skis." My cousin Geoff was nineteen and fearless. In the last two months I'd seen him jump off of the roof and into the pool, climb a tree so high I could no longer see him, and do flips and all sorts of frightening tricks on his water skis and wakeboard. Truth was, he was stressing me out, and I wasn't in the mood for another anxiety induced stomach ache.

I finally set down my crayon and sat back to examine the end results.

"And?" My mother studied my expression as she came to sit beside me with a plate of cookies and a glass of milk.

I took a cookie and dipped it. "I'm not sure yet."

"What aren't you sure about?" She waited for me to remove my cookie before she went to dip hers as well. This was standard cookie ritual for us. No need to waste an extra glass of milk that no one was ever going to drink. It was strictly there for dipping purposes.

"If the dress is long enough."

She leaned over to get a better angle of my art work. "Is this a wedding dress?"

9

I nodded. "Uh-huh." I reached for my purple crayon and started on the bouquet.

"Who's getting married?" My mother smiled as if she already knew.

"Me and Emerson." I didn't even look up.

"You and Emerson? Don't you think he's just a little bit too old for you?"

The thought had occurred to me. Especially ever since Spence and him had started hanging out with some girls they met who were staying in a house just up along the water. Emerson hadn't ignored me exactly, but I'd definitely noticed his heightened interest in the other girls. Even at six, jealousy was a very real thing.

Mostly, I just didn't think those older girls really appreciated all of the wonderful things about him. Sure, I'd heard them giggling about how cute he was, but what did that matter?

At my age, you didn't fall for a boy because of how he looked, although he was certainly dreamy by my standards. Or, at least, that's what I liked to tell myself. In all reality, I wasn't entirely sure what it was that made him so dreamy or why that was important in the first place. I did know that Emerson would spend hours sitting beside me on the docks, waiting for me to catch a fish, even when everyone else had already had their fill of fishing. I knew that he held my hand when I got scared on our outdoor expeditions and that he never complained when I insisted on squeezing in between him and whoever was sitting beside him at the dinner table. As far as I was concerned, Emerson was the coolest and funniest person I'd ever met. And it just made sense to me that someday, he and I would wind up on one of my mother's presentation boards, because as far as I knew, every boy and girl did at one point or another.

"I'm not getting married *now*." I may have been young, but even I knew that was ridiculous.

"Oh, okay. Just checking." She leaned into her seat, taking another bite of her cookie. I got the distinct feeling she was laughing at me, although I couldn't see it.

"Mommy?" I reached for my green crayon in order to add stems to my purple flowers.

"Yeah, baby."

"When do you think I *would* be old enough to get married?" I purposely kept my eyes down on my paper, feeling suddenly embarrassed.

"Well, technically, you can get married when you turn eighteen, but take it from me, that doesn't always work out as well as you think it ought to. So, how about twenty-five?"

That sounded like a million years from now.

"But what if he marries someone else before I'm old enough?" I lifted my head to face her. This was a serious concern.

My mother nodded a few times, as she thought it over. "You know, I think I have a solution." She stood from the table and left the room. A few moments later, she walked back in, holding several cards in her hand. "Do you remember what these are, Lissy?"

I did. "They're save the date cards, so people don't forget their wedding."

She chuckled. "Close. They're so other people know that they're going to be invited to a wedding. This way they don't forget and make other plans. But I think today, we could use them your way. You could make two. One for you and one for Emerson. We can pick a date nineteen years from now and write it on the cards. That way, you'll both remember to wait and not marry anyone else."

And so that's exactly what I did. By hand and with my mother's help, I filled in both cards very carefully. She even let me use her fancy gold marker to do it. When I was done, I stuck mine into my scrapbook right beside the picture I'd drawn.

"Are you going to give the other one to Emerson?" my mother inquired curiously.

"Not yet." I pressed the card to my chest, slid out of my chair and strolled out of the room.

I waited until the very last day of our vacation. Then, when it came time to say goodbye, I went to find him.

"Staring contest. Go!" I peered up at him, trying my hardest not to giggle as he stared straight back, never even flinching. Finally, I couldn't take it anymore, I succumbed to the laughter bubbling up from inside.

"I win," he called out triumphantly.

"Fine." I gave my best impression of an angry face. "Then I guess you get a prize." I reached under my t-shirt and pulled the card from where I had wedged it between my stomach and the waistline of my pants. It had been too big to fit into any of my pockets.

"What's this?" He took the unexpected card and flipped it over several times. It was sealed in a lavender envelope which I had aptly bedazzled in every shade of glitter my mother had given me access to.

"It's just so you don't forget." Then I wrapped my arms around his waist, said goodbye and went to find my parents outside in the driveway waiting for me.

Seems that knowing the Ashcraft family has been shaping my life in different ways for as long as I can remember. Growing up had meant living in and out of my mother's car for the most part. Shelters when it was too cold to sleep in the old Chevy. After leaving my father for actions that should make any woman walk out, her options had been limited and for reasons I was too young to understand, she was unable to seek out traditional employment. And so, it wasn't until I was eight that she was able to find a job as a live-in nanny, as well as a more suitable home for us with Ross and Lindy Ashcraft and their three children, Simon, Spencer and Savannah.

From then on, life was a new kind of a wonderful. Our state of poverty and the Ashcraft life of luxury had been opposite ends of the spectrum and for some inexplicable reason, they had seen it fit to extend their good fortune to us from the moment we set foot in their front door.

Things had only gotten better when I discovered their son, Spencer, was the same age as I was. And, in the years that followed, we had grown up to be best friends. Brothers even. So, it was no surprise to anyone when I was invited to come along on family vacations, including the ones at the family lake house on Lake Kentucky.

Later on in my twenties, when I had managed to mangle my life all on my own after my mother's passing and was in desperate need of a job, it had been the Ashcrafts who came through for me yet again. Even more so than just a way to make some money, they led me to my passion. The thing I would do for the rest of my life, and I knew nothing else could ever trump this gift that they had given me. Until I was thirty-three and I realized that something else already had, years ago, at the lake house.

Chapter 1

"Are you done yet?!" A wave of steam hit me as I threw open the bathroom door.

"Does it look like I'm done?" It did not.

"Hurry up! I need to be at work in less than thirty minutes and it's going to take me fifteen just to get there!" I wiped the mirror with my sleeve to assess my hair. Nope. Skipping the wash would not be an option.

Suddenly the shower curtain flew back.

"You could always join me." Any other day the sight of Tyler standing there with water droplets pearling on his perfectly smooth skin, light dancing in the dew as he flexed his muscles, would have been a welcome image. Today, I just found it annoying.

"That is it! From now on, you can't sleep over anymore," I yelled as I stormed from the bathroom.

I was barely two feet back into my bedroom when I nearly tripped over Tyler's shoes. I picked them up and hurled them into the nearest corner. "And pick up you stuff! A girl could get killed in here!"

Tyler and I had been dating for nearly a year now, and up until recently, things had been amazing. Then, out of the blue, he had decided it was time to take our relationship to the next level. So, before I knew it, he had brought over a box of his things and I had been forced to vacate a drawer for them.

If you knew me, and I mean, knew me *at all*, you would know that there are two things I cannot stand. One, being late and two, someone messing with my stuff.

Blame it on the fact that I'm an only child. Blame it on me being a total control freak. I don't care. Either way, I was not fond of the idea of having to move all of my belongings over, which now suddenly had nowhere to go, just so he could have a place to keep his underwear and spare phone charger. To make matters worse, one drawer never seemed quite enough.

All of a sudden, he was adding shoes to my closet. Hanging extra towels on my towel rack. It was like he was freaking moving in.

"It's all you." He stood there, dripping water on my hardwood floors. It was all I could do not to choke the living daylights out of him. Instead, I closed my eyes and silently counted to ten.

"Listen. This isn't working. I realize this is a total cliché, but - It's me. Not you. I can't take it. I'm just not cut out for a real relationship. It's making me crazy. And what's worse, it's making me hate you."

I handed him a towel while he stood there completely dumbstruck. "Do me a favor and wipe up the floor. I really need to get in the shower."

By the time I got back out, Tyler was gone. So was all of his crap.

I got to work twenty minutes late. I barely had enough time to stop in my office to grab the sketches I needed and then run all the way to the presentation room in the back where the meeting had already started without me.

I was about to knock and let myself in, when my assistant Stephanie came at me, outstretched hand yielding a hot and delicious coffee.

"Oh my God, Steph. I love you," I whispered. Now her I would let move in, in a heartbeat.

I took one quick sip and then braced myself for what was waiting on the other side of the door.

"Good morning, Calista Joy. So nice of you to join us." Even at my age, you knew you were in trouble when your mother used your middle name.

"So sorry I'm late. I had an unforeseen circumstance. Either way, I apologize for keeping you all waiting."

This was our fourth meeting this week with the bride-to-be and today she had brought along a whole new slew of people. The wedding itself was only three months away and nothing had been finalized as of yet. Not even the dress. I'd provided her with seven sketches in the last six months and she had found a problem with all of them. I had two more for her today. After this, I was making an appointment for her at Kleinfeld's.

These issues weren't uncommon for brides with limitless funds. I think it's the feeling of knowing the sky's the limit and worrying they'll miss out on something even better than what they've already seen that overwhelms them. Regardless, it was annoying, not to mention stressful. But I kept my mouth shut.

At twenty-three I was the youngest dress designer in the city. I'm sure most people assumed that my extensive client list stemmed solely from working in the confines of my mother's shadow, but the truth was, I had talent.

Sure, my mother's connections had granted me opportunities early on that most designers only dreamed of. Starting at sixteen I was spending my summers doing internships with all the big names in bridal wear. At eighteen, I even ventured off to France for a bit before coming home to start school at Parson's.

Once I graduated it seemed stupid not to take my mother up on her offer to set up shop in *her* shop. I was in need of a job and she had been wanting for some time to add 'custom bridal dresses' to her list of services. It was a win/win.

Except on days like today, where it felt like we were all losing.

"I'm not sure how I feel about this neckline. I thought I would like it better this way, but now that I'm seeing it with the full skirt, it just doesn't look right." Madison, our bride, was scrunching up her nose like a piglet. Her rosy cheeks and strawberry blonde hair were doing nothing to offset the visual. Nor was it helping that I kind of *wanted* her to look like a pig at that point. Or a cow. Really, any farm animal would have done the trick.

I watched as she flipped back and forth between the two new sketches, shaking her head and distorting her face in a variety of expressions, one more unsightly than the next while the women sitting to either side of her mimicked her every move.

"I'm sorry, I'm just not feeling like these are for me, you know? I mean, they always say, when you finally find the right dress you just know." She handed the sketches over across the table where I carelessly slid them back into my folder. I had known they were hideous all along. Pretty sure I had told her they would be when we discussed the changes she wanted me to make.

"Completely understandable, Madison. And that's absolutely true. Finding your wedding dress is always love at first sight. When you see it, you always know." I reached down into my bag and pulled out another sketch. It was a ballsy move, but I had nothing to lose at this point.

"I may have one more for you. It's a design I was saving for my collection. I was actually considering planning the entire line around it, so I probably shouldn't even show it to you..." The moment I placed it in front of her, Madison's eyes lit up.

"OMG! This is it. This is my dress," she squealed loudly, eagerly showing the image to all of her friends.

It was the first sketch I'd ever drawn for her. She had shot it down in two seconds flat two months ago, but now, it was *the one*.

Once the whole dress debacle was finally over, my mother was able to finalize all of her plans as well. Suddenly, Madison had no problems making any decisions. Everything my mother suggested sounded perfect to her and all she did anymore was nod and smile, all the while never even taking her eyes from the sketch of her dream gown.

In spite of how annoyed I'd been with her these past months, there was no escaping the high that followed anytime a bride fell in love with a dress that I'd created for her. There was something absolutely amazing about knowing that I'd played a part in bringing someone's childhood fantasy to life. And let's face it, that's basically what weddings are. A childhood fantasy. Only unlike the ones we had about jumping off of rooftops and soaring through the air like Superman, we're actually dumb enough to pursue this one.

In case you hadn't noticed, I had extremely mixed feelings when it came to marriage. On the one hand, I'd clearly dedicated my life to love and the elusive, possibly imaginary, happily ever after. On the other, I was a jaded, love hating cynic who wasn't about to fall for any of that crap herself.

"So, what was the unforeseen circumstance today?" My mother was standing in the open doorway to my office, casually sipping what I could only assume was some plain organic tea of one flavor or another. More than likely it was green or chamomile. I made a face just thinking about it.

"Tyler. But not to worry. It won't happen again." I reached for my coffee, my second cup of the day. God bless Steph. She'd had it sitting on my desk waiting for me as soon as I walked in after that torturous meeting.

Her curiosity piqued, my mother came all the way in and had a seat on the sofa along the back wall. "And why exactly are you so sure it won't happen again?"

"Because I broke up with him." I made sure to sound as casual as possible. As of yet, no unpleasant feelings regarding the sudden break up had surfaced and I was hoping to keep it that way for as long as possible.

My mother just shook her head. "What was it this time, Cal?"

"You were there, you already know. He's the reason I was late." If that wasn't reason enough, I didn't know what was.

"You, my darling daughter, have commitment issues." She laughed at me as she stood up and began to leave.

"Oh, this coming from the woman who hasn't been in a relationship in seven years." Maybe even longer. As far as I knew, there had been no one since the divorce.

"That's because I'm perfectly happy being committed to myself." She smiled that 'I'm your mother and I know everything' smile and then walked out.

She was barely out of the room when my phone started blowing up. Tori. She and I'd been friends since first grade. More importantly, Tyler was her boyfriend Kyle's older brother. She'd set us up herself and had no doubt been planning our double weddings and baby showers ever since. I didn't have to read a single one of her text messages to know what they were about.

Seven jingles later and I bypassed reading and simply hit call.

"You don't break off a year-long relationship with someone while they're standing there completely naked. It's not fair. It makes the dumpee vulnerable and it's just bad manners, Cal!"

"First of all, he was not naked he was wearing a towel, and second of all, don't even get me started on bad manners. I can assure you, when it comes to practicing proper etiquette, Tyler does a sub-par job at best. I have two stains on my hardwood floor the shape of his feet caused by water damage this morning to prove it." I didn't know why I was even bothering. I'd never win this one anyway.

"What if he was the one, Cal? What if he was the one and you threw him out because he got your floor wet?" This was ridiculous.

"He wasn't the one, Tor." I rolled my eyes knowing she wouldn't be able to see it and reached for my coffee. It was cold. Between my mother and her, a perfectly innocent cup of heavenly brew had gone to waste. I shook my head in disgust at their recklessness.

Meanwhile, Tori ranted on, "How do you know? How do you know he wasn't the one? He could have been."

"No Tor, he couldn't have been."

"How can you be so sure?"

"Because if he had been *the one* he would have known better than to hog the shower. He wasn't the one."

I could hear her grumbling things to herself. I didn't have to be able to make out the words to get the gist of it. This was hardly my first lecture. For as long as I could remember, Tori had been obsessed with one thing and one thing only – falling in love. From the time we were eleven I had spent every Sunday evening planted on her sofa, watching some ridiculous Hallmark movie or another. Then when we turned thirteen, things got a little more intense as she added boy bands and that guy from the OC to the mix. It's fairly safe to say, Tori has been boy crazy since before she was old enough to appreciate the benefits of having one.

I, on the other hand, was always a bit more reserved in this area. Maybe because I grew up in a home where love was a convenience and not a passion. Or maybe just because Tori had the whole thing covered already for the both of us. Either way, while she was busy fantasizing about the way Kyle might propose to her one day, the only weddings on my mind were those of my clients.

"Do you still need me on the line for this or can I get back to work?" I had two more meetings to prepare for and I wasn't remotely ready. I was already going to have to work straight through lunch as it was.

"Why can't you just be a normal girl for once in your life, Cal? What is so wrong with falling in love and living happily ever after? Do you really want to be alone forever?"

I dropped the stack of files I had pulled from my drawer onto my desk, making a loud clapping sound in the process.

"Who said I was going to be alone forever? I'm twenty-three, Tor. And this is the twenty-first century. It's fine if you want to get married and settle down. But don't act like it's insane for me to be single right now. I've got shit to do and I'm not wasting my time on some asshole who's going to hold me back. Even if it is just by making me late for a meeting."

I could hear her sigh loudly on the other end. A clear sign of surrender. Except I knew it was only temporary.

"Fine. Go do you."

"No one else does it better."

"See you Sunday?"

"Of course." As I said it, I made a little note reminding me to check the TV listings for this weekend's movie. Over the years I'd learned that most of them fell into three basic categories – single mom meets troubled stranger and falls in love, work-a-holic/ jaded woman falls for the silent but strong country guy, and last, but certainly not least, the sweet innocent girl meets sweet innocent boy, but due to massive miscommunications and odd misunderstandings, they don't actually wind up together until three minutes before the movie ends. This category tended to always come equipped with some sweet senior doling out advice to the innocent ones, which somehow made it more bearable than the other two. Those in turn required a great deal more chocolate to endure and I wanted to be prepared.

When I finally got Tori off the phone, I dove right into sketching. Aside from Steph popping in to drop off a veggie and hummus platter from the deli downstairs, I didn't see or speak to anyone until I was done, at which point I found myself having to make another run for it down the hall as I was showing up late for my second meeting of the day. *Stupid Tyler*.

"Hey Burke, you wanted to see me?" I was standing in my boss's office.

"Yeah. How long have you been workin' here now, you think? Seven, eight years?"

It was nine. "Something like that. What's up?"

"Emerson, how old do you think I am?"

It was an odd question and I sure as shit didn't want to answer it. But I did. "Old, Burke. You're goddamn old."

He laughed. "Hell yes, I am. So, how much longer you think you're going to need before you can start takin' over so I can get some rest?"

I frowned. "You thinkin' about retirin'?"

"No, I'm not thinkin' about it. I'm doin' it. Already talked it over with everyone, and we all agree, there's no one better than you." Burke stood up from behind his desk and held out his hand. "You've got six months kid. Then it'll be all you."

Speechless, I met his hand with mine, and we shook on it. I was six months from having it all.

Chapter 2

With Tyler plucked neatly from my life again, I spent my Saturday in silent solitude only interrupting the quiet every so often to hum to myself as I went about straightening up my room and returning my belongings to their original, and now vacated, places. The truth was, part of me had been looking forward to this moment. Had been counting down the days until the other part of me, the part that enjoyed having Tyler around, finally came to the dark side and sent him packing so that life could go back to normal.

If I was completely honest with myself, knowing that I'd felt that way the entire time scared me ever so slightly. Sure, I was always quick to set Tori straight when she made the argument, but there were times I wondered if she was right. What if I really did end up alone? I liked being on my own, but I hated being lonely.

Come Sunday evening, I was happy to head over to Tori's, even if it was to spend two hours watching a movie that would likely make me want to stuff my face with chocolate just to keep my endorphins elevated.

"Ooh, what's in the box?" Tori was already closing the door behind me and hurrying to catch up as I wandered straight down the hall and into her living room.

"Cake samples. My mom's trying out a new bakery." I placed the large cake filled carton on the coffee table and plopped down into Tori's overstuffed sofa. It was ridiculously comfortable.

25

"God I love your job!" This coming from the girl who spent her days in a recording studio meeting one music icon after the next. Tori's father had spent the last three decades becoming a well accomplished producer before branching out and starting his own label. And, much like myself, Tori hadn't strayed far from the family business.

"So, no Kyle tonight?" I glanced around the room rather obviously. It wasn't exactly official, but Tori's boyfriend had more or less been living with her for the last six months. The only thing keeping it in its state of limbo were his extremely religious parents. I had met them shortly after Tyler and I had started dating and then had been banned from ever returning two minutes after walking through the door when their German Shepard had run over, diving nose first into my crotch causing me to drop the f-bomb in shock of it all. I mean, seriously. Who wouldn't feel inclined to have a little verbal outburst after having been molested by a ninety pound dog?!

Anyway, official or not, Kyle was definitely spending the majority of his time at Tori's. And, judging by the stack of mail I passed on the way in, word was getting out.

"Kyle's out with Tyler trying to cheer him up."

"Why? What's wrong with him? Something happen?"

If Tori's mouth hadn't been full of red velvet cake just then, her jaw might have dropped all the way down to her knees. She swallowed hard, forcing down the sticky sweetness. "Yes, something happened! You dumped him, remember?"

Oh, right.

"Come on, he can't be *that* upset about it." Surely he had seen it coming. I mean, I certainly had.

"Yes, he's upset about it. Look, I wasn't supposed to tell you this, but just last week he was with Kyle...at Tiffany's." She was giving me that look. That, 'why aren't you getting what I'm telling you it's so obvious a five year old would get it' look.

"Shut the fuck up. Are you telling me Tyler was going to propose?" Talk about dodging a bullet.

"Yes! Why are you taking this so lightly?" Tori's exasperation was showing in more than just the fact that she had now completely abandoned her cake. She was pacing and looked like she might punch a wall...or strangle me. Considering she was only 5'1 and *maybe* weighed a hundred pounds, I felt fairly safe even in spite of the murderous rage beginning to glimmer in her icy blue eyes.

"Hey look, our movie's starting." I hastily reached for the remote and turned up the volume in hopes that I could force her into silence by simply drowning her out. It worked. Begrudgingly, she came to plop down beside me. She didn't utter so much as a single word for the next two hours, but resorted to staring daggers into the side of my head during each commercial break. I didn't care. I'd had seventeen years of experience already.

After two torturous hours of sickeningly sweet romance and way too many samples of cake, I laid sprawled out on the sofa like a beached whale; too full and too depressed to move. It wasn't like I wanted any of what I'd just seen. It was more like I wanted to *want it*. I just didn't. And I hadn't for a long time. Maybe ever. No, not ever. I had wanted it once. But I had been six, so that probably didn't count.

"You're right. Tyler wasn't the one." Tori grumbled as she slowly peeled herself up off of the cushions.

"Excuse me?" After all of that she was just going to pull the ol' switch-a-roo on me?

"Look, if Hallmark has taught us anything, it's that fate is an unwavering, uncompromising and unstoppable force. If you could toss Tyler from your life on a whim and feel absolutely zero emotional backlash, fate was clearly not a factor."

See, I knew I'd been right. "Honestly. I expected some to come this time. It just didn't." I glanced up at her, "Sad, huh?"

"Not sad." She shook her head. "Normal. For you anyway."

"Oh, that makes me feel loads better. I'm some non-feeling freak incapable of love."

Tori picked up one of the couch pillows and dropped it on my face. "Don't be an idiot. You're capable of love. You love me."

I tossed the pillow across the room. "Some days."

She grinned. "Most days." Then she reached down and grabbed my hands to pull me up. "Come on. No more basking in the glory of your state of utter patheticness."

"Patheticness is not a word, Tor." I reluctantly came to my feet.

"Is now. Been used in a sentence twice already."

I couldn't help but laugh. Then I noticed she was collecting my belongings and bringing me my shoes, which I had flipped off and kicked in two different directions about halfway through the movie. "Wait, are you throwing me out?"

She made a face. "Kyle will be here soon. He's still kind of pissed about the whole you dumping his brother thing. Just give it a week or two and it won't be awkward anymore."

"Tori!" Instinctively I snatched up what remained of the cake. "I'm your best friend!"

"You *are* my best friend. But he's my boyfriend, and unlike you, I like having one of those." She playfully nudged my elbow. "Besides, I know you'll love me no matter what."

"Some days," I grumbled as I slid my feet back into my shoes. Peep toe pumps with three inch heels. They'd seemed like the perfect choice this morning. Now the thought of having to walk even as far as the front door seemed less appealing than walking barefoot over shards of glass.

Clearly seeking out redemption, Tori handed me a pair of flip-flops and smiled. "Most days."

No longer worried about my bad choice in footwear, walking seemed like a viable option as I stepped outside and felt the chill of the evening air run over me. It wouldn't be long and the enjoyable evening air would turn hot and humid. Tonight, it was perfection.

First chance I got, I ditched the big box and, with no other alternative, ate the last piece of cake with my hands as I walked along the empty sidewalks.

I was almost back to my place when I felt my phone vibrate in my pocket.

"Hey Ma."

"Movie night over already?" I could hear jazz playing softly in the background. In all likelihood my mother was sitting curled up on her chaise lounge, sipping a nice Shiraz and reading the newest Nora Roberts novel.

"Yeah, got booted out early since Kyle's not my biggest fan right now."

"I see. Well, I'm calling because I have some news. Your cousin is getting married."

I shoved the leftover paper wrapper from my cake sample into my purse and nodded at Sam the doorman as I walked into my building. "Which cousin, Ma? You'll have to be a little more specific."

She laughed. "Sorry. It's Savannah."

"Um…who is she again?" Horrible, I know. But I hadn't seen any of them in nearly two decades.

"You remember Savannah. She's just a couple years older than you. Spencer's sister."

Spencer. Emerson.

"Oh okay, now I know." She and I had been closest in age. She'd be twenty-five now. I guess it wasn't a real big shocker she was getting married. Although, I couldn't recall ever getting a call to notify me of any of my other cousins' nuptials. I seriously doubted they were all still single. So, what was making Savannah's engagement so much more newsworthy?

"They've asked us to plan the wedding."

Ah. Now I understood. "Sounds like fun. When is it?" I was just turning the final corner in the hall toward my apartment.

"In two weeks."

My hand froze just as I was about to put my key into the lock. "I'm sorry, what now?"

"The wedding is in two weeks. Which means, we have no time to waste. I've already booked you a flight. You leave first thing in the morning."

"What are you talking about? She doesn't need *us* to plan a two week wedding. She needs David's Bridal and Party City. And why am I the only one with a flight?"

"Because I can get started from here, but you can't. Besides, someone needs to go into the office tomorrow to make all of the necessary arrangements for our business to survive while we leave town for a while."

I regained enough self-awareness again to successfully unlock my door and go inside. Shaking my head as I went through the motions of dropping my keys in the basket in the hall, and flipping on the lights as I made my way to the kitchen for a bottle of water, I went on, "I still don't understand what the urgent urgency is here. I mean, even if she's pregnant, we're talking like a three month window to put together a hidden belly celebration."

"Savannah isn't pregnant. The reason it's so last minute is because their original wedding planner up and ran out of town with the groom-to-be set to marry one of her other clients. As it turns out, the affair had been keeping her pretty occupied. So much so that she dropped the ball on several other weddings. Savannah's included."

"Oh. How very Young and the Restless they are down in Kentucky. I'm not gonna lie. I'm a little scared to go down there now. Who knows what kind of scandal I might find myself in!?"

"Calista don't be ridiculous. It's the south. It's not a soap opera." There was a clinking sound as the wine bottle hit the rim of her glass mid-refill. Apparently, I was driving my mother to drink. "Look, I know you've never had the chance to be very close to your family, and that's my fault, but Savannah is your cousin and invitations were sent out weeks ago. We can do this for her."

I sighed. "What time?"

"The car will be there at six in the morning. I trust Tyler is still a goner and you will be on time?"

"With bells on." I twirled my finger in midair even though no one was around to appreciate the sarcastic gesture.

"Perfect. Well, I'll let you go then. You've got some packing to do."

"Night, Ma."

"Good night, Cal."

"What's up, Spence?" I opened one eye to check the clock. It was almost three a.m. One day Spencer would realize that I got up every day at the crack of dawn, and therefore was generally asleep during the hours he deemed best to call me.

"Just talked to Savannah for like two hours. If ever there had been a time to wish the ER got hit with a massive car wreck. Or a gang shoot out, or something. Shit. There was nothing. Not so much as a fucking hang nail walked in the doors. So I was stuck listening to her about some drama with her wedding planner. She was so fucking hysterical the whole time I only understood about half of it. Any idea what that was about?"

I reached out and fumbled around on my nightstand until I found the light switch. Then, blinded by the sudden light, I pulled myself up into a sitting position, realizing this might take a while.

"Listen, Spence. Before we go any further, you do realize that it's the middle of the night and unlike you, the med school survivor who learned to exist without the time for sleep, I actually require a little shut eye every now and then. I know I don't have to operate on anyone when I go to work in the morning, but I think we can both agree it would be detrimental to my physical well-being if I fell asleep on the job." I took a moment to see if he would answer.

"Shit, sorry man. It's like a Las Vegas casino up in here. I never know what fucking time it is anymore."

"No worries. Anyway, back to Savannah. She's got her panties all in a wad because there's some rumors flying around town about her wedding planner being involved in some sort of scandal. And that's not all. Apparently, she's closed up shop. As of this moment, there's no wedding."

I could hear Spence coughing. Probably choking on whatever energy drink he was chugging down. "What do you mean there's no wedding? I got my invite weeks ago. I had to jump through hoops to get it off."

"Yeah, and I'm sure those are all really valid concerns, but I wouldn't mention them to your sister anytime soon since she's on the verge of having what was supposed to be the most important day of her life, blow up in smoke." I pulled back the covers and let my feet drop to the floor. There'd be no point in going back to sleep after this conversation.

"You said on the verge. So there's still hope?" There was more noise on Spencer's end. Rustling sounds. Probably a bag of Doritos or something. For a doctor he had an almost embarrassing diet.

"I guess. Your grandmother's supposed to call your Aunt Sophie. See if there's anything she can do. I mean, she's like the fairy Godmother of weddings, right? So, I'm sure it will all work out…in the end. We'll all just need to wear ear plugs to drown out Savannah's screeching in the meantime. And we probably shouldn't be too surprised if random dogs start followin' her around. They'll be pickin' up on that high pitch of hers."

Spencer laughed. "I'll be sure to point that out to her next time I talk to her."

"Please do."

I hung up and headed for the shower. There was bound to be something to do back at work.

Chapter 3

Trying to pack for Kentucky had been an absolute nightmare. I must have packed and unpacked and then re-packed my bags at least five times. Every time I thought I had the perfect combination of work attire and Ashcraft Farm attire, I'd second guess myself and start over. And rightfully so. Not only did I not have a clue what farm attire might consist of, I was also quite certain that I didn't actually have any articles of clothing suitable of that description in my wardrobe.

I was about to say fuck it, when I remembered that Kentucky was likely experiencing some warmer conditions than we were this time of year. One quick Google search later and the weather site had confirmed my suspicions. That's how round number five of the packing game came to be.

By the time I was finally finished, attempting to go to sleep seemed pretty pointless. So, I pulled the trusty laptop back out of its travel case and began to cyber-stalk my mother's side of the family. It was research for work of course. Finding some current pictures of Savannah would mean being able to mentally start preparing for the type of dress she might want. Naturally, body shape and overall look played a large part in coming up with the right design.

An hour and a half of scouring through Facebook and clicking on every name that ended in Ashcraft later, and it was finally time for me to wander downstairs to the lobby where Sam was already waiting to take my bags and load them into the car my mother had sent for me.

It was lunchtime when I landed in Lexington and I was starving. Unfortunately, it wasn't until I was walking out through the arrival gate that I realized my mother hadn't expounded on what I would be doing once I arrived.

Was someone meeting me? Was I supposed to take a cab? If so…would they know where to go if I just said 'to Ashcraft Farms, please'? I was in the process of speed texting my mother in a low blood sugar induced mania, when I heard it.

"Sweet baby Jesus, there she is. Oh lord, would you look at her? All grown up and lookin' just like her Mama. Can you believe it?" Noonie Skeeter. Also known as my grandmother.

Given that half of her statements had been formed as questions, I looked up expecting to see Poppy with her. He however, was nowhere to be found. Neither was anyone else. Noonie Skeeter was all on her own and running over toward me as fast as she could, her arms flying at me and ready to rope me in.

With both arms pinned down at my sides and my face being smothered in kisses which were likely leaving behind thick traces of my grandmother's bright coral colored lipstick, I stood there helplessly waiting for the flood of love coming at me to subside.

"Hi Noonie."

"Oh, baby, it's so good to see you! And in just one more day, your Mama will be here too and I'll have all my babies in the same place again. Lord, does it get any better than that?"

She glanced up, quite literally asking the big guy upstairs. Caught up in the moment, I waited, compelled to hear him answer. And he might have, although I hadn't heard him. Noonie Skeeter seemed to have been satisfied with the response though as she happily hooked her arm into mine and began walking me through the airport toward the baggage claim area, all the while, chatting about a gazillion different things pertaining to a slew of people I couldn't even begin to place.

Twenty minutes later and I was sitting in the cab of her massive Dodge Ram and holding on for dear life as she zipped in and out of traffic as though she were driving something the size of a mini cooper. Suddenly, not having eaten lunch yet had worked out in my favor. Or, in Noonie's favor, depending on how you looked at it.

I did my best to keep up with the conversation, but mostly all I could do was stay on top of my nodding and insert polite laughter whenever there was an awkward pause that deemed it necessary. Then, before I knew it, we were pulling in through the huge wrought iron gates.

I remembered the first time I'd ever seen them. It had been the same summer I'd been to the lake house. At six, the gates had seemed massive. Hell, at twenty-three they weren't much smaller.

Whatever preconceived notions I'd had about the family farm had been wiped away with the wind that came whistling down over the endless rolling hills of green pastures that made up Ashcraft Farms.

See, the name 'farm', while perhaps appropriate in the state of Kentucky, was more than just a little misleading to a young girl from the city. Where I had foolishly believed that my grandparents owned a place chockfull of chickens and cows and everything in between, their farm was actually less of a farm- farm and more of a multi-million dollar race horse breeding and training facility. Easy mistake to make, of course.

The last time I'd been back to Ashcraft Farms had been nine years ago, the Christmas after my parents divorced. I think my mother had needed an escape at the time, and Kentucky certainly made it easy to disappear. No one from Manhattan would have a snowball's chance in hell of finding anyone there. Not with all the open spaces to get distracted by. And God forbid if they stopped to ask anyone for directions. It'd be like watching two aliens from opposite galaxies attempt to have a conversation.

As far as I could tell, not much had changed since I'd been fourteen. Which was comforting in its own way. At least while feeling out of place, I'd still have a vague sense of being somewhere slightly familiar.

Once we made our way up the long winding driveway to the house, Noonie Skeeter parked the truck and we got out. Three big dogs came running over to greet us. They were definitely new. There'd been dogs last time, too, but they'd been smaller with slick hair. These reminded me of bear cubs with their bushy fur and stubby tails.

Noonie took the time to greet each and every one of them while also introducing them to me.

"The two black ones are ours – Spot and Bubba – I know," she shook her head and rolled her eyes back into her head, "Poppy named them." Then she pointed over at the third one, a ball of brown and tan fur. "That one there's named Reesie, on account of her lookin' like a Reese's Peanut Butter Cup. She belongs to one of our trainers. She's sweet as can be and here just about every day."

I nodded, making a mental note of all their names. "Got it." Then, I followed her up the steps of the front porch and into the house. Well, mansion was more like it. Or was it considered an estate? Beats me. Either way, the place was huge. So, huge I couldn't help but think one of those 'you are here' maps would've come in handy on every floor. And there were three.

We ran into Pattie, the housekeeper, who greeted me with a warm hug like any surrogate grandmother would, just outside of the kitchen. We didn't find Poppy until after we went up a flight of stairs and wandered into his study.

"Well, hello there darlin'! Ain't you a sight for sore eyes." He came out from behind his desk and squeezed me tight.

"It's good to see you guys. It's been a while." God, how lame. But what did I say? Sorry, I suck as a granddaughter? I blame my mother? If it helps, I hardly see the Luvalle side either and they just live three short blocks from me? That last one might have actually not been half bad. Although, it did sort of reiterate the point of the first one, and I didn't come off too well in that excuse.

"A long, long while." Poppy stepped back and gave me the standard once over every older relative seemed to give, assessing the progress I'd made in growing up since they'd last seen me.

"Now, I know you're here to help Savannah with her weddin', but I don't want you to be all caught up in work the whole time, ya hear? I understand you city folk enjoy a high paced lifestyle, but while you're here, I want you to slow it down a bit. Take some time to enjoy and relax."

Clearly Poppy had never planned a wedding. With a preparation time of two weeks, there would be no such thing as enjoying or relaxing. There would hardly be eating and sleeping.

"Alright, Poppy." I smiled my best polite smile. "Speaking of the wedding, is Savannah around? I really need to sit down with her so we can get some dress ideas going."

"Savannah will be by later this afternoon. In the meantime, how about we get you settled in?" Noonie was already taking my arm and leading me from the study and down the hall.

At the very end, she opened a door revealing a gorgeous guest suite fully equipped with everything a girl could need to survive, including a gigantic tub with whirlpool jets sitting right there in the bedroom beside the fireplace.

"Wow. I didn't stay in this room last time I was here," I mumbled as I went to set down my purse beside the rest of my luggage which had magically already arrived at the room. Well, Pattie-ly was probably more like it.

"You were quite a lot younger last time you were here. This is a big girl room." Noonie Skeeter winked as she walked out and closed the door behind her.

Already feeling like I might melt if I didn't shed some of my layers, after only having been in the southern sun for mere minutes out in the driveway, I went straight for my suitcase and opened it up. Normally I loved my clothes. And I mean, *looooved* them. Today, I hated every single item I owned for its impracticality. Sure, back home my wardrobe was useful, but here I hardly had use for any of my high fashion items, and would likely destroy them if I even ventured outside of a three foot radius surrounding the house.

This left me with a collection of well-worn jeans and my underwear. Not exactly ideal either. Oh well, first things first. I slid my feet from of my crème colored pumps and stripped out of my jasmine sleeveless crepe cady and lace jumpsuit, along with the matching straight leg trousers. Instantly, I felt better.

I pulled several dresses from my suitcase and laid them out across the bed where I stared each of them down for a long time until deciding that not a one would work. Not for now anyway. I went ahead and took the rose colored, short and flared organza dress with the embroidered flower details on the front, and hung it on the bathroom door for later. It would work nicely for sitting down with Savannah once she showed up to talk wedding plans. In the meantime, I had some time to kill, and the stables were pulling at me to come and see the spring foals. Given my limited visits, I'd never been here at the right time of year before to see them for myself, but even in my mother's random stories of the past, she'd mentioned the foals on more than one occasion and I was eager to have a peek at them myself.

It pained me to do it, but I finally admitted defeat and resorted to ripping apart one of my less favorite blouses until I was left with something that almost resembled a tank top. At last I had something to pair with my jeans. While I was at it, I went ahead and had a rip at them as well, quickly turning them into a cute pair of cut offs.

This of course still left me with bare feet. Since there was no way I'd be wearing any of my shoes into the barn, I wandered out into the hall in search of Noonie Skeeter.

I found Pattie instead.

"Hey Pattie. I don't suppose there's a spare pair of boots lying around in some closet somewhere? Something around a size eight maybe?"

Pattie smiled. "Follow me."

So I did. All the way back toward Poppy's study and up the final set of stairs up to the third floor. I couldn't remember ever actually having been up there before. Pattie stopped at the second door in the hall and went inside. The room was a fairly decent size with three windows lining the main wall. It was nice, although extremely dated and decked out in all things horse.

"Whose room is this?"

"This was your mama's room. You ain't never been up here?"

I shook my head. "No. Are you sure this was her room?" It looked nothing like her. Not a single thing in this room reflected my mother in any way. At least not, the version of her that I knew.

Pattie just chuckled and went on to the closet in the corner of the room. I half expected a cluster of moths to come flying out when she opened the doors, or bats even. However, neither was the case. Instead, Pattie retrieved a pair of old cowboy boots and handed them over to me.

"These ought to fit." She gave my elbow a light squeeze as she went by me, leaving me behind in a room that was almost starting to give me the creeps.

I couldn't put my finger on it, but it had the distinct feeling of someone or something having died in it and a part of me suspected it was in some way related to the reason my mother had rarely ever spoken of her family for as long as I could remember.

Not surprisingly, the boots fit damn near perfectly. Much like most of my mother's shoes which had mysteriously found their way into my closet over the years.

I walked through the large house and out the front door without running into a single soul. I'd probably have to get used to that while I was there. Once outside, there seemed to be a great deal more life around, although, it was predominantly four legged and covered in fur. But I didn't mind. Company was all the same to me.

While Bubba and Spot quickly got distracted and ran off into one of the surrounding pastures, Reesie remained glued to my side and accompanied me all the way down to the main stables.

It was quiet when I walked in. Aside from the random snort or shuffle of hooves as they moved through the thick layers of straw and saw dust, there wasn't much else to be heard. Tentatively, I moved along the stalls, peering in on every horse I passed in search of babies, but there were none to be found.

Disappointed, I was about to turn back and move on to the next barn when I heard a voice from behind.

"Excuse me. Can I help you?"

Slightly startled by the deep and raspy tone of the man's voice, I spun around. The light from the sun was shining in through the open doors behind him, making it impossible to get a good look at the man's face. His body however was another story. Between the sun's bright rays and the dark shadows of the barn aisle, he was outlined perfectly. And I do mean, *perfectly*. Between his broad shoulders, muscular arms and lean but solid chest, it didn't much matter *what* his face looked like.

"It's fine," I finally said after an awkwardly long silence. "I mean, I'm fine. Skeeter and Troy are my grandparents."

The guy took several more steps in my direction. Suddenly the light adjusted and I could see his face. It had aged some. His hair had turned from its rusty brown to a dark chestnut. It was longer and shaggier and accompanied by a day's worth of matching stubble along his jawline and chin. The only remnants of the boy he'd been were left in the fiery sparkle of trouble still blazing in his brown eyes. Emerson.

"Holy shit. Lissy?"

I laughed. "Yeah. But no one's called me that in years."

"Wow. I mean, damn." He was shaking his head, still looking me up and down as he walked over, and I could feel the heat rising through my cheeks straight out of the top of my head. "You probably don't remember me, but I came up to the lake house with your cousin Spencer one year."

"I know who you are, Emerson."

He nodded, a pleasantly surprised look on his face as he came to stop just a few feet in front of me. "You've grown up some since the last time I saw you."

"Well, I was only six…so yeah. I had some growing up to do." I crossed one leg in front of the other and folded my arm behind my back, clasping my other arm just so my hand would have something to do. It wasn't lost on me that as I was declaring my state of adulthood, I was suddenly standing there like my six year old self again. All that was missing were my standard pig tails and a lollipop.

"I guess so. And I hear you plan weddings now?"

I teetered back and forth from one foot to the other, keeping up my childish posture and silently berating myself while doing so. "Oh, no. I don't plan them. I dress them. I'm a designer. I do custom wedding dresses." A simple 'I design the dress' probably would have sufficed, but it was too late now. Meanwhile, I had to suck in my lower lip and bite down on it, just to keep from rambling on any further.

I didn't understand what was happening. Sure. Emerson was freaking hot. But, come on! This wasn't like me. I didn't come completely undone just from standing face to face with a guy. Even if he did have the most

44

beautiful lips I'd ever seen sitting right there above that perfectly chiseled jaw. *Oh God. Don't smile.* Too late.

"Did you have anything to do with that shirt you're wearing?" He was still grinning as he lifted his hand to reach for the edge of my sleeves where I had ripped off an impractically flared bit of chiffon earlier. The tips of his fingers grazed my skin as he did so and I had to swallow hard before answering.

"I might have made a few adjustments here and there. It's not my best work." I grinned back at him, desperately hoping he hadn't noticed the effect he'd had on me. In the meantime, I was still gently swaying back and forth to keep my legs from going numb, or worse yet, giving out on me all together. Holy crap. What was going on?!

"Well, it still looks good on you, but then I imagine just about anything would."

Wait a minute. Was he flirting with me? Before I had a chance to come up with a clever and coy response, he went on, "So, what brings you out here all alone?"

I shrugged. "I was hoping to see the spring foals. And, I'm not alone. Reesie came with me." I pointed at the chocolate colored fur ball rolling around in what bore an unfortunate resemblance to horse manure.

"Oh, so she's been hanging out with you. I was wondering where she went off to." He knelt down and Reesie instantly abandoned her enjoyable roll to run over and greet him.

"She's your dog?" I don't know why I was so struck by the news. "So, then you work here? For my Grandparents? You're a trainer." There I went again, spitting out chopped up chunks of conversation like a poorly programmed robot.

"Yeah. Been working here for a few years now," He stood up, dusting whatever had transferred from Reesie's coat to his hands off on his pant leg. "Come on. Foals are out this way." Then, without hesitating, he took my hand and led the way outside.

I had to take several fast steps in a row to keep up with him as his long legs took wide strides through the barn and then out and around the back to a wide open pasture.

There they were. At least six or seven little guys. They were adorable with their long gangly legs and bushy mane and tails. A couple of them were running around playfully, but most of them remained glued safely to their mother's shoulder.

"This what you were hopin' for?"

"Uh-huh." I just stood there, staring out at them and bursting with a new sense of delight. "Thank you."

"My pleasure. Anything else you want to see? I could give you a whole tour if you'd like." Emerson had both arms resting on the wooden slats of the fence and was comfortably leaning into them.

I was about to respond, when my stomach interrupted me with a loud howl. Mortified, I grabbed my belly button as if I could silence the beast within by doing so.

"We should probably start with the kitchen." He laughed as he took my hand again, tugging me along as if I was still the same little six year old from that summer at Lake Kentucky.

When we got up to the house, Emerson walked in without even knocking. I couldn't help but think about how weird it was that he felt more at home at my grandparents' house than I did. I probably would have rang the doorbell and then waited for someone to answer.

But he just kept walking, straight through the foyer and the formal dining room to the back where the kitchen was. He was about to push the swinging door open when he caught a glimpse of Pattie moving through on the other side through the long narrow window neatly placed in the center of the door.

Instinctively he leaned back and reached his arm across my midsection, gently pressing me against the wall and out of sight. He lifted his finger to his lips to signal me to keep quiet and I did. I was starting to think they had some weird fucking habits around here, but I enjoyed being in such close proximity to him way too much to question it.

After a moment, he lowered his arm, flashed me a broad smile and headed into the kitchen.

"So…was that like a southern thing? Or are you actually an escaped mental patient who just thinks he works here but in reality will get hauled off in a straitjacket on sight?"

He chuckled. "It's a Pattie thing. She's very possessive of her kitchen. If she knew you were hungry, she'd pull out all the stops and you'd be sittin' here for the next three hours having food shoved in your face."

He reached for both handles on the double door fridge and pulled. The thing was huge, much like everything else around here, and filled with more food than my fridge had ever seen in the three years I'd owned it.

"I don't see where having food coming at me for several hours is a bad thing. You heard my stomach. It's been a while…"

Emerson somehow managed to retrieve several items without disturbing the rest of the contents. I watched as he set them all down on the butcher block island at the center of the room.

"It wouldn't be a bad thing, just not a convenient thing."

I went over to one of the bar stools and had a seat on it. "What would be so inconvenient about it?"

He was just in the middle of throwing together a combination of meats and cheeses on two slices of fresh whole wheat bread when he looked up. That same flash of playfulness flared up in his eyes. "The part where you'd be stuck in here, while I'd be out there thinking of all the more fun things we could be doing." He placed both halves of the sandwich together and held it out to me. "Here. This ought to hold you over until supper."

"Thanks." I stared at the collection of deli products smashed between the bread, completely dumbstruck by what was happening. Aside from the fact that I'd never seen a sandwich quite like this one, I couldn't recall a single time any guy had ever made me one. The most I'd ever seen a man do in the kitchen on my behalf was start the coffee maker, and generally that had been motivated by selfish reasons.

Emerson finished cleaning up after himself and came back to stand in front of me. "You going to eat that or just stare at it all day?"

"It's so big, I don't think I can fit it in my mouth."

"Yeah, I've heard that before. About my sandwiches." His lower lip was twitching as he fought back a smirk.

"Oh my God, Emerson! Innocent ears over here."

He just grinned, placed both hands outside of mine and pressed them together, flattening out the sandwich in the process. "There, should be able to fit it now." He winked at me and went to lead the way back out of the kitchen, hooking one finger into my belt loop as he went by and dragging me along while I giggled like a little girl.

God, she's gorgeous. Wait. Am I allowed to think that? This is little Lissy Luvalle. Little Lissy with the pig tails and the big brown eyes that made you say yes no matter what the question was. Well, she sure as hell isn't wearing any pigtails now. But damn. She still has those eyes.

Chapter 4

I devoured my late lunch in a matter of minutes. By the time Emerson came to a stop, I was just wiping the last crumbs off my hands.

"So, where are we and what are we doing?" I was looking around, a little nervous at the sight of our destination. From the looks of it, Emerson had dragged me out to an old shed. Inevitably the escaped mental patient theory made a reappearance. Thankfully, Reesie had followed along and I was counting on her to have my back. Even if she was technically his dog.

"You'll see." He really wasn't helping matters any. Emerson opened the rickety old door and went inside, disappearing in the darkness. A moment later, he emerged. Two fishing poles in one hand and a tackle box in the other. He nodded to the left. "Come on. Water's this way."

He was several feet ahead of me already, when I jumped into motion as well. "Wait. What water?"

Instead of answering, Emerson just gave a forward wave, reiterating the fact that he wanted me to simply follow along. And, without questioning it any further, I did. Guess I figured if my mother had thought I was in good hands with him when I was just a child, I'd probably be fairly safe now as well. Not to mention that my grandparents had seen fit to hire him.

Although halfway through hiking around in some marshy dark woods I began to second guess my mother's judgment. As well as my grandparents'. I was about to announce that I was heading back out to where I could actually see daylight, when our path cleared and I found myself at the edge of a creek.

With the warmth of the sun dancing on my skin again, and the quiet babbling of the moving water, it was really quite lovely.

It was clear that Emerson had been down here plenty of times before from the way several logs had been positioned to provide a nice little seating area. Immediately I wondered who else had sat there with him as I lowered myself down onto the log beside him.

He rummaged around in his tackle box for a second and then held out a jar in my direction. It was filled with worms and I recoiled at the sight.

"Oh no. That is so not happening." I held out my hand, trying to force the jar away without having to actually touch it.

"I know you know how to hook your own worm, Liss. I know, because I remember teaching you how to do it." Before I could stop him, he grabbed my outstretched hand, turned it over and placed a squiggly pink worm in my palm.

For a moment I thought the sandwich I'd eaten in such a haste would come back up just as fast as it had gone down.

"You're really making me do this? I thought you said we were going to have fun." I made a face, still holding my hand out away from my body as if the little worm might jump up and attack me with its grossness.

Emerson smirked as he stood up, his rod ready to go. "I am having fun."

"Yeah, I bet you are," I grumbled as I grabbed my fishing pole and threaded the line in my fingers until I found the hook. Then, after lining it up with my worm, I closed my eyes and did the thing I was dreading most. Surprisingly enough, baiting your hook was very much like riding a bike. Once you began the motions of it all, everything came right back and I opened my eyes to find my poor worm perfectly pierced and ready to go as if I'd been doing it every day since Emerson first taught me seventeen years ago.

Feeling quite impressed with myself, I came to my feet and looked up. Emerson was staring at me, a peculiar expression on his face.

"What?" I placed my free hand on my hip defiantly. No way was he going to knock my baiting efforts. Not after I didn't even want to do it in the first place.

"Relax, firecracker." He reached out and hooked my belt loop again to pull me over beside him. "You squeezed your eyes shut like that when you were six, too, you know that? You don't crinkle your nose anymore, but your aim has improved considerably."

"I didn't used to crinkle my nose!" My mind instantly conjured up images of flared nostrils and a variety of unattractive expressions I'd rather hadn't seared themselves into Emerson's memory for all eternity.

"Sure you did. Spence and I would sit there watching you bait your hook with your eyes closed and wait for it. Right as you pressed the worm into the point, you'd crinkle that little nose. Happened every time, without fail. It was adorable. Kind of bummed you dropped it from the routine."

I couldn't tell if he was making fun of me or flirting again. Although, the fact that he kept comparing me to my six year old self was more than a bit disheartening. Maybe some part of him would always see me that way.

Why do you care?! Why indeed. Sure, Emerson was annoyingly attractive, even if he wasn't remotely like any of the guys I'd dated in the past. But, did his hotness have to translate into anything more than a simple attraction? Did I want it to?

I finally cast my line and then settled in and waited for the fish to bite. More than once I caught myself trying to peer up at him out of the corner of my eye, which led to silent cursing over the fact that I hadn't thought to put on my sunglasses prior to leaving the house. Not that it was all that bright, but they certainly would have aided me in trying to gawk at the man standing two feet away without him noticing.

As it was, I limited myself to glances below the waist which could easily have been mistaken for interest in the flowing water or the random wildlife that scurried around the banks along the river.

The view wasn't too shabby. For starters, Emerson had hands and arms that made you want to be gripped tightly by them. And not in the friendly, he gives good hugs sort of way, but in the throw me up against a wall and maul me kind of way.

They were strong, working hands which gave the distinct impression of knowing what they were doing, no matter *what* they were doing. In spite of the near perfectly tan skin that stretched tightly over his muscled arms with each flick of the wrist as he moved his line in the water, there were small patches on his forearms and hands. Old scars from doing, well, to be perfectly honest, I could only speculate at this point. What exactly did one do on a farm? Regardless, in my warped and silly mind, scars represented something dangerous, which in turn translated to bravery which naturally brought me back full circle and being pinned up against the wall.

"So, tell me, what has little Lissy been up to in the last seventeen years? I mean, aside from getting into the bridal business."

The sound of his voice snapped me back to reality where I found myself staring quite inappropriately, and not entirely discreetly, at the man's groin area. If he saw me doing so, he didn't let on.

Attempting to sound as casual as possible, and to hide my overall flustered demeanor, I replied, "Oh, you know. A little of this…little of that."

He turned back to read my expression. "What exactly are this and that?"

I had no idea.

"I just mean, I haven't been doing anything out of the ordinary." Bullshit. Nothing about my life had been ordinary. Why the hell was I insisting on selling myself short?

Emerson's brow scrunched together curiously. "Really? That's not what I hear."

Now it was my turn to be curious. "Why? What have you heard?"

"Well, according to your grandmother, you've been quite the go-getter. And not just as a designer, but also as a real estate mogul. To hear her tell it, you've been kicking ass and taking names."

"Well, I wouldn't go that far, but sure. I suppose you could say I've been unusually successful for someone my age." I felt a quick tug at my line and went to reel it in. The pressure ceased instantly and I knew what I'd find as soon as the hook broke water. "Damn." The worm was gone. I'd have to start all over.

Emerson leaned his pole up against a large boulder along the waterline and came to sit beside me while I proceeded with my baiting routine.

"Must keep pretty busy with so much going on. How do you make time to just sit back and enjoy life?"

"I like being busy. Besides, the real estate thing isn't so much a business as it is my father's idea of daddy daughter time." It was true. After the divorce he'd been at a loss concerning the whole parenting thing. Suddenly without my mother to back him up and tell him what to do, he didn't seem to have a clue as to how to fill the time he had to spend with me come every other Friday. So, he'd done the only thing he knew how to do. He'd taken me to work. "We never really had much in common. His way of fixing that was to teach me all about the thing he loves, real estate. Guess it was easier than trying to get to know his teenage daughter."

I was trying to make light of it, but judging from Emerson's expression, he had set aside the joke and zoned right in on the heart of the matter.

"Sounds like your dad's missing out."

"Maybe." I looked down at the innocent little worm lying curled up in the palm of my hand. Then, casually, I turned it, letting him slide down into the dirt below. "Truth is, it's better this way. With the relationship we have now, I know exactly what I've got. I have something I can depend on. And it's a lot less heartbreaking this way." I smiled wryly. It had been a long time since I'd talked to anyone about my dad. Maybe ever.

Emerson watched me thoughtfully for a moment longer as if he was contemplating whether or not to continue to pursue the conversation. Then, apparently thinking better of it, he tilted his head to the side, the mischievous look returning.

"Well, we don't seem to be having much luck here. Let's get going. I've got a better idea."

He jumped up and went to retrieve his pole.

I stayed seated on my log a second longer, mumbling, "I'm afraid to ask."

"You'll like this. Promise," he chuckled and before I knew it, we were back in the woods making our way to the rickety old shack of a fishing shed.

After dropping off our gear, we headed back down toward the main barn. I felt a bit of panic set in.

"Um, you do know that I don't know how to ride, right?" I felt like I was bringing shame to the Ashcraft name just by saying the words out loud.

Emerson nodded. "Not to worry. I'll teach you." Then he looked back at me, "But not today."

The relief was short lived as I began to wonder what else he had up his sleeve. How much could there possibly be to do around here? When I saw him approach an old pick-up truck I concluded I'd been on the right track with my thinking.

"Wait, I can't leave. Savannah will be by soon."

"I know." He was doing that all-knowing cocky grin thing. It was aggravatingly sexy.

"Then what's with the truck?"

He held the door open for me. "Climb in and find out."

Reluctantly, I slid into the seat. The passenger side was filled with lead ropes and other random items I didn't recognize but assumed were in some way horse related, leaving me no choice but to sit awkwardly in the middle, unable to avoid having various parts of my body touching his.

As I continued to try and keep myself in my own seat, Emerson seemed completely unaware. If anything, he seemed to spread out further, repeatedly brushing my knee with his hand as he shifted gears on the old stick shift.

When we reached a gate, he jumped out to open it before hurrying back to drive through and then run back to close it again behind us.

"You know, you could have just asked me to get the gate."

He shook his head, laughing softly. "You've been hanging around with the wrong kind of men, Lissy."

"Maybe *you* need to hang around with some more capable women," I huffed.

"It's not about that. A gentleman doesn't do what he does because he thinks a woman needs him to. He does it because he wants to." Then he turned to face me. "And you really ought to learn to let him."

Maybe he was onto something.

I kept my mouth shut the rest of the drive and enjoyed the view. We were slowly cruising through another pasture. This one had at least twenty or so horses in it. They looked young, but considerably older than the foals he'd shown me earlier.

When we reached the top of a small hill, Emerson stopped the truck and got out. Then he held out his hand for me to take and, in spite of my instincts not to, I took it.

Together we walked to the back of the truck where he lowered the tailgate and promptly grabbed me by the waist and hoisted me on top of it.

I was about to make my argument for capable women again, when he climbed up as well and gestured for me to have a seat on the hay bales he had loaded in the back.

To my surprise the hay was quite soft and it smelled amazing as I leaned into it. The only thing more wonderful than the scent was the view. Emerson had strategically parked the truck in such a way that we could see the entire farm from where we were seated.

"Wow. This is beautiful."

"Well, I did promise you a tour of the place earlier, so…" He lifted his arm and pointed over to the far right corner nearest to the road. "That right there is one of our equipment barns. It's the largest one we have on the property and it's where we keep all of our large tractors and such."

I nodded. "So, it's a garage."

He smirked. "Sure. Then, straight across the front of the property you see the training tracks which consist of a 1 1/8-mile main track, a 7/8-mile turf track and a one-mile, L-shaped jogging track, which borders the main track."

"So knowledgeable. You sound like such a proper tour guide. Do this often, do you?"

This time he just ignored me and went on as if I hadn't interrupted again.

"Over to the left are two barns, both containing thirty-six stalls each. This is where we keep the horses in training. Not all of them are ours. Many of them come here just to use the facility." He shifted his weight and pointed at a thick cluster of trees beyond the stables. "Which is why we have several guest houses on the property straight through that wooded patch. Back there is also where you'll find Burke's house and some homes for some of the other full-timers."

I nodded. It took me a second, but then I remembered. Burke was the barn manager. "You live back there, too?"

Emerson shook his head. "No. I've got a place just up the road." Then he went back to giving me his tour without skipping a beat. "You already know the broodmare barn and clearly you're aware of the main house. We've seen several pastures and been down to the creek, which really only leaves the round pens and walkers over that way. And then of course, the last of the stables."

I took it all in. The few times in my life I'd actually been here, no one had ever taken the time to explain to me what everything was. Maybe they just assumed I wasn't interested. Or maybe they thought I just wouldn't understand. Either way, they'd been wrong and I was grateful to Emerson for finally sharing with me what my own family hadn't.

"It's stunning, isn't it? I mean, Manhattan is gorgeous. The architecture, the ambiance, but this, this is breathtaking."

He bumped his knee against mine. "I told you, you'd like it."

"And you were right." I beamed up at him. After all this time, Emerson hadn't changed at all. He was still the same patient and kind person I'd been so enamored with as a little girl. Only this time around, I had a very clear idea of what it was that made him so incredibly dreamy.

Watching her sitting there beside me with the sun dancing on her long brown hair, all I could think about was touching it. Curling it around my fingers, feeling the soft strands as I ran them through my hands. I still couldn't believe I was sitting there with the same little girl who had followed me around all summer all those years ago. Only there was nothing little about her. Lissy was all grown up. And not just physically. Listening to her talk, I was caught off guard by how mature she was. Liss was smart. From the sounds of it, she'd already figured out more at twenty-three than I had by the time I was thirty. Not to mention her accomplishments, which put mine to shame even now. But not for long. Soon. Soon, even I would have something to offer to someone like her. Although I could hardly imagine why she would want it.

Nevertheless, there was something about being with her. It was comfortable. Easy. Exciting. And nothing had excited me this way in a long time.

Chapter 5

I have no idea how much time we spent sitting out in the middle of that field under the warmth of the afternoon sun, but somewhere along the way, all thoughts of Savannah and her wedding had been completely forgotten. Thankfully, Emerson had spotted her Jag coming up the long winding driveway and had gotten me back down to the main house moments later.

Rather than come in, he simply dropped me at the front door and went on to other things. Guess he did officially have a job to do around here and it likely wasn't to keep me entertained.

I could feel a glow on my skin as I stepped inside the air conditioned house. The onset of a tan I hoped.

I was about to begin a thorough search of the house for Savannah when I heard a loud squeal coming from the stairs.

"Calista!" She was running, skipping steps as she went until she was close enough to fling both arms around me, jumping and giggling as she dragged me around in excited circles which were quickly making me dizzy.

"Hey Savannah." Even after not having seen her in nearly a decade I would have recognized her anywhere. She was an Ashcraft through and through with those big blonde locks, bright blue eyes and pointy little nose. Not to mention she had the trademark Ashcraft dimples and the voluptuous curves all the women seemed to have been blessed with. Well, all except one. Yet another reason to make me wonder just how the hell I wound up sharing a branch with everyone on this family tree. I didn't possess a single one of those traits. Although my mother certainly did. Guess I was more Luvalle than Ashcraft. At least in the looks department.

When she finally let me go, she took a step back, still holding onto my wrist and gave me a dramatic once over. "Damn girl. Look at you all grown up. And I'm lovin' this city meets country thing you've got goin' on! Wait 'til the boys 'round here get a look at ya. They'll be all tongues pantin' and tails pointin'."

"Holy shit, you southerners are crude. That's the second penis reference I've heard today."

"Just tellin' it like it is, darlin'." Savannah giggled in that cute feminine way I'd never quite mastered. I'd told myself I'd rather die than giggle that way, but truth was, I felt a pang of jealousy anytime I witnessed a successful delivery. Naturally, it always came from someone who was already overflowing with all things lady-like. Even if they were talking about erections while doing so.

"Well, I don't know about all that. I do know that you're gonna be scraping your groom's jaw off the ground by the time I have you walking down the aisle. Come on, I sketched some stuff on the plane I want to show you." I headed for the stairs and gestured for her to follow.

Once upstairs in my room, we had a seat on my bed. I pulled my sketchbook from my bag and began to flip through the pages.

"How'd you end up without a dress anyway? I mean, I know your wedding plans got tossed by the wayside by that rogue wedding planner, but didn't you do any dress shopping on your own?"

Savannah nodded dramatically. "Sure did. It was gorgeous, too. Most beautiful dress you could possibly imagine – well, scratch that, it probably doesn't apply to you – but it was definitely the most beautiful dress *I'd* ever imagined."

I looked up from my pile of papers. "Then what happened to it?"

"That bitch stole it! I mean it. She just stole it right out from under me, same as she did that groom. Of course, she didn't come right out with her thievin'. No, she was way too clever for that. She was there when I bought the dress, so she knew I needed a few modifications made on account of my waist bein' so tiny and my chest bein', well, less tiny. Anyway, she insisted I let her take the dress to her seamstress. Said she was the best in all of Kentucky and I didn't want to take any chances with a dress that stunning. Ha! Seamstress my ass! After she took off, I searched hell and high water for this mysterious seamstress only to find out she didn't even exist. So, now here I am, two weeks before my wedding and I've got no cake, no venue and no dress." Thoughtfully she reached for the sketches in my lap and began to skim them. "Suppose things could be worse though. I mean, that other bride wound up with no groom."

I laughed dryly. "Yeah, that would be worse." I pulled my feet up and crossed them in an attempt to get more comfortable. "Speaking of, who's the lucky fellow anyway?"

Without taking her eyes from the images in her hands, she said, "I don't know how lucky he is. He's been telling me what a pain in his ass I am for as long as I can remember."

"You two grew up together?" My heart was starting to race and I didn't even know why.

"Not exactly. He grew up a great deal sooner than I did." She did the giggling thing again. "He's my big brother's best friend."

No. I could feel the blood draining from my face as she happily chatted on. "Let me tell you, it wasn't easy gettin' him to see me as girlfriend material. Although, these babies certainly didn't hurt." She pushed her arms together, pressing her breasts upward, just in case I hadn't understood what she'd meant by 'these babies'. Rest assured, I had.

"Well, I guess he came around, huh? I mean, now that you've graduated to 'wife material'." I was trying my hardest to sound happy for her, but the truth was I was pissed. How the hell had Emerson just spent all afternoon with me and never once mentioned that it was *his* wedding I had come to town to help plan? Didn't that seem like a pertinent piece of information? Who the hell neglected to share something like that?

From there things only got worse when my anger faded and transformed to humiliation. What an idiot I'd been, thinking he had actually flirted with me. I was just as delusional now as I'd been all those years ago when I'd convinced myself that Emerson and I would end in our own little happily ever after. Really, had he treated me any different today than he'd treated me back then?

I glanced up from my internal meltdown to see Savannah holding up one of the tentative gowns I'd drawn up on the plane.

"This one. It's so sexy and classy. Can you really make me a dress like this in time for the wedding?" Her eyes were full of desperate hope.

I took the drawing to see which dress she'd chosen. It was a slimming mermaid silhouette with crystal hand-beading which framed the plunging V-neckline and sheer cap sleeves. Lace appliqués and more scattered beading would highlight the sheer back bodice, which I'd designed complete with cascading crystal buttons to conceal the zipper closure. A scalloped chapel length train finished off the stunning gown. I wasn't surprised she liked it. I did my best work under pressure and a gown like this would hug her curves in all the right ways. Emerson would surely appreciate it. The thought alone made me want to rip the sketch to shreds.

Instead I nodded confidently. "Absolutely. If this is the dress you want, then this is the dress you shall get. But you don't have to pick one from the stack. I'd be more than happy to draw up something from scratch for you. I just thought I'd show you these to give you some ideas of what I can do and what I imagined might suit you."

Savannah reached over and repeatedly pointed at the paper in my hands. "No, this one. This one, just the way it is. It's perfect. In fact, it's even more perfect than the dress I had. I oughta send that thievin' bitch a thank you card."

I grinned at my cousin. I couldn't even stay mad at her. It wasn't her fault I'd temporarily gotten lost in my childhood fantasy while she'd grown up and created herself a more permanent reality.

"If you're sure, then let's get this show on the road. I'll need some measurements from you and then a vehicle of some sort to get into town so I can start acquiring the needed materials."

Savannah's eyes got wide. "You mean to tell me, you're going to actually *make* this dress yourself?"

"Well, yeah. Who did you think was going to do it? Think I packed a bunch of dress elves in my carryon?"

She snorted. A serious contrast to all the delicate giggling she'd been doing. "No, I guess not. I just…you can do that?"

"I can do that." I nodded slowly, not sure where the hang up was with the whole thing. After all, this was what I did for a living. It was this precise skill that had landed me on a plane here in the first place.

"I don't know. I guess I just thought you came up with the design and then…outsourced it."

"I do, back home. I've got a small team I work with. But, that doesn't mean I don't do any of the sewing. I did go to school to learn how if that's what you're worried about."

Savannah shook her head, clearly concerned that she had offended me. "Oh, hun, I'm not worried about a thing! Now, let's get these measurements out of the way so we can go shopping!"

Thirty minutes later I was strapped in the front seat of Savannah's Jag holding on for dear life as she zoomed through the streets.

Although the fabric stores weren't quite what I was accustomed to, we still managed to find just about everything we needed. The rest I'd have my mother bring when she came into town the following day.

"Now then. Since we've got my dress all figured out. What are your thoughts on the bridesmaids?"

I stared at her with eyes so wide she probably thought they were about to pop straight from their sockets. "What do you mean, what are my thoughts on the bridesmaids? Are you telling me they don't have dresses either?"

Savannah laughed, not at all fazed by my sudden panic attack. She reached out and placed her hand on my arm in what I suppose people around there thought was a kind gesture, but what people from where I was from considered to be an invitation to being bitch slapped. "No sugar, of course they have dresses."

I sighed, relieved. Too soon.

"But those were intended to go with my former gown. I'm afraid they aren't at all suitable now."

"Savannah! I'm good, but I'm no fucking miracle worker." I closed my eyes and took a deep breath. "Okay. Just get me a list of your best bridal boutiques and I will get us in to look at some stuff. If I need to add some customized touches, I will. But you have to make sure you get all of your bridesmaids there when I say so. Got it?"

She nodded gleefully.

Then I remembered the one thing that hadn't come up yet. "How many bridesmaids are we talking anyway?"

I watched as Savannah's head shrunk down into her shoulders as she squeaked, "Eleven."

"I'm sorry, what now?" I was absolutely convinced that she was fucking with me. After all, who would have eleven bridesmaids? Who even had that many girlfriends? I could hardly string together three. And I had to count Stephanie, my assistant, to do even that.

"There are eleven bridesmaids. With me, that makes an even dozen. If it makes you feel any better, I had thirteen but decided to let two of them go when I found out they were both sleeping with the same groomsman."

"You run a tight ship." Sarcasm was the only weapon I had to utilize at this point. Savannah, however, took me completely seriously.

"Oh, well, I had to. His wife is one of my bridesmaids as well and it would have been one big mess trying to get all three of 'em down the aisle without a big catfight breaking out."

"Yeah." My eyes were threatening to escape their sockets again as I slowly nodded my head in disbelief. This was going to be one hell of a wedding.

By the time Savannah dropped me back at Ashcraft Farms, it was way past dinner. In our haste to get everything purchased before the stores began closing, we hadn't even thought about food. Now, as I was wandering through the quiet house peering into the dimly lit rooms with no signs of life other than the quiet hum of a television stemming from one of the upstairs bedrooms, I was doing more than just thinking about food. I was fantasizing about it. Willing it into reality and into my mouth by any means necessary.

With Pattie absent, I quietly made my way toward the kitchen. I came to a dead stop the second I stepped inside. There, in the light of the open fridge, stood none other than Emerson.

"What are you still doing here? I thought you lived up the road." It came out about as snotty as I had intended it to.

Startled, he turned around. Then, when he realized it was just me, he broke into a broad grin. "Haven't had time to go grocery shopping in a while. Besides, when I came through here earlier I could smell Pattie's famous barbeque ribs. Been craving some ever since."

He placed a large glass pan covered in aluminum foil onto the counter. "You want some? What am I saying? Of course you want some. You just spent the afternoon shopping with Savannah. You're bound to be starving." He laughed as he opened the top cupboard to fetch some plates.

Suddenly my appetite was gone. "Why? Does shopping with her make you hungry?"

He paused for a moment, a funny expression on his face. Then he set the plates down beside the ribs and prepared himself a heaping serving. "I make it a point never to go shopping with Savannah."

I was surprised. For some reason I imagined Emerson saying yes to doing just about anything Savannah's little heart desired. He'd certainly said yes to every silly thing mine had requested of him in the past. "Doesn't that bother her?"

He shrugged. "Why would it? She has plenty of shopping buddies around. I seriously doubt she needs to recruit me to be one of them."

What an ass. "Well, I'm sure she does things for you that she doesn't enjoy." *Like dealing with your slut of a groomsman who can't keep his married dick in his pants for example.*

Emerson had a mouth full of pork when he replied, "I wouldn't know what."

Men were so freaking oblivious.

"Whatever. I'm going to bed."

"Did I do something to piss you off?" His brow was knitted, showing his confusion over my attitude.

How did I even answer that? Oh, right. With a lie. "It's not you. I'm just tired."

Before he had a chance to say anything else, I hurried from the room, my gut twisting in hunger and anxiety as I went.

Holy shit. Talk about blowing it in record time. I had obviously done something to upset her, didn't matter that she denied it. Even I wasn't that oblivious. Maybe Savannah would tell me. I just needed to find a casual way to ask her. If she thought for even a moment that I was interested in her cousin, I'd never hear the end of it.

Chapter 6

The following morning, I got ready in a hurry, eager to catch a ride to the airport with Noonie Skeeter to pick up my mother. Not that I was desperate to see her after only having been gone for twenty-four hours. It was more out of desperation not to see anyone else for a while. I had made enough of an ass of myself the night before in the kitchen with Emerson and I wasn't looking for a repeat anytime soon.

If I could just have some time to recollect my thoughts and over analyze my feelings, I was positive I could re-route my childhood crush in a new and healthier direction.

The drive went by in a bit of a blur. After skipping dinner the night before, the thought of food had made me nauseous first thing in the morning. Instead, I had opted for a large cup of coffee. And then a second right after. And of course, a third for the road.

Now that I was flying high as a kite on sugar and caffeine, I found myself in a state of delirium as I watched the scenery change outside of my window.

"I noticed you and Emerson were spending time together yesterday." The sound of Noonie's voice ripped me right out of my happy place.

"It was nothing. He was just showing me around since I hadn't seen the place in a few years." Well, ever, really.

"That was nice of him." Noonie looked like she had more to say, but she simply kept her eyes on the road ahead and her mouth shut.

"Yeah, I guess it was." I returned my focus on the view outside my window.

Apparently, Noonie Skeeter reconsidered. "He's a good boy, you know. Does a finer job with our animals than anyone I've ever seen. Sometimes I wonder though if it's at the expense of his people skills."

I snorted, remembering how clueless he'd been the night before in the kitchen. "There might be something to that theory, Noonie."

"Now you be nice to that boy, Calista. He's got more kindness in his heart than he knows what to do with. Too many people have tried to scare it out of him already, don't you be one of 'em, too. He may not always show it the way you or I would, but he does it in his own way."

It was the first time I'd ever been scolded by her. Incidentally, I wasn't entirely sure what I'd done to deserve it. She certainly had a soft spot for Emerson. Which I suppose made sense. My mother always said her horses were her greatest love, so if Emerson was doing right by them, he'd be doing right by her in every way that counted.

"Noonie, I'm nice to everyone. Even socially stunted country boys."

She shot me a dirty look.

"Alright, alright. I'll be nice."

"Now that's better. And just in time. We're here."

A few minutes later and we were walking from the parking garage and into the main terminal. My mother's flight had arrived early, so she was bound to be buzzing around somewhere, sipping one of her disgustingly healthy teas and filling up countless shopping bags with useless crap she'd find use for somewhere along the way.

I was about to suggest we check in the nearest souvenir shop when a familiar smile caught my eye.

"Stephanie? What are you doing here?"

"Your mother sent me. Said you might be able to use a hand. There was something about a dozen bridesmaids?"

"She knew?!" Unbelievable. Kind of made me wonder what else she had held out on.

"I guess. She said not to worry about anything else. Everything is moving full speed ahead with the wedding plans and she can't wait to get here and join in on all the fun."

I snorted. Fun was definitely an overstatement on her part. "And when exactly will that be?"

"Um, in two or three days. A week, tops." Steph was smiling at me uncomfortably. It was for nothing though. I wasn't in the habit of shooting the messenger. It was a waste of bullets and I preferred to save mine for the real target.

"I can't believe she's weaseling her way out of this!" I was amping up to have a proper rant when I realized Noonie Skeeter was standing beside me, silently waiting for the standard introduction. "I'm so sorry. Steph, this is my Grandmother. Noonie Skeeter meet my assistant Stephanie."

Steph extended her hand immediately. "So nice to meet you Mrs. Ashcraft."

"Oh, sugar, call me Skeeter. Everybody does."

"Alright then, Skeeter it is."

I watched as Steph's face did a slight twitch at the sound of her own voice saying my grandmother's name. You didn't meet a whole lot of people named Skeeter up north. Hell, I wondered how many people still went by that name down south. My Noonie was certainly the only person I'd ever met who went by Skeeter. Of course, it suited her better than any name I could have come up with.

"Now then, I see you already have all of your luggage," Noonie Skeeter said pointing at the overflowing cart Steph was tugging along behind her. "No more reason to stay around here any longer than necessary. Besides, Pattie's back at the house fixin' pulled pork sandwiches for lunch as we speak. I don't know about you two girls, but that's about all the motivation I need to get back home." She didn't wait for either of us to answer. Just smiled that crazy crooked grin of hers and started walking. Steph and I had to hurry to catch up, both of us carting the trolley behind us like a pair of driving horses.

"I take it most of this crap belongs to my mother?" I huffed from the strain.

"She said they were important wedding supplies. She even sent one of those fancy collages for your cousin. Also, one of the bags is full of *your* crap." Steph was smirking, in spite of her clear discomfort. How she had managed to cart this thing around on her own was beyond me. But it did explain the beads of sweat on her forehead and the unusual red tone in her cheeks when I'd first seen her.

"Hey, I'm not the one who made you bring it. I fully expected my mother to be the pack mule lugging this load. What's the real reason she bailed anyway?" I kept my voice down, just in case. Noonie Skeeter struck me as the type of woman who wasn't about to let a little thing like age dull her senses. If anything, I suspected her hearing improved over the years.

Stephanie shrugged. "Not sure. To tell you the truth, I don't know of any pressing matters back at the office that would keep her there. I even talked to Jack, her PA. He was just as surprised as I was that I was coming in her place." We reached the front doors and stepped outside into the warm sunshine. "You know, I think he was a little peeved about the whole thing. He was supposed to be coming out here as well to help your mom."

I grimaced. "Well, if my mother ever makes it out here, I'm sure she'll have him in tow. She doesn't do much of anything without him these days. Sometimes when she calls me in the evenings, I picture him there at her place with her, pouring her wine and giving her a pedicure."

Stephanie and I both erupted in giggles and they were nothing like the cute kind Savannah engaged in.

Much to my annoyance, the first thing we saw upon pulling into the long drive of Ashton Farms, was of course, Emerson. To make matters worse, he looked like he had jumped straight out of that Legends of the Fall movie as he rode by on his horse wearing a well fitted work shirt, and a severely worn and weathered cowboy hat which shadowed over an expression of cocky confidence with a troubled undertone à la Brad Pitt, minus the long hair.

"Helllllllo," Steph muttered to herself.

I leaned in toward her. "He's taken."

Noonie Skeeter had the distinct traits of a smile dancing on her lips, however it never fully formed and I wasn't sure if she had heard us or not.

Once inside the house, Noonie informed us that there was a second guest room just two doors up from the one I was staying in. So, four trips later, we were both sitting on the floor in Steph's suite digging through all of the bags my mother had sent with her.

"So, who's the cowboy?" Stephanie was retrieving pile after pile of swatches from a satchel which Savannah was meant to search through at some point to choose a suitable color for her table linens.

"The groom actually. His name is Emerson. He's been a friend of the family's forever. First time I met him I was just a kid. He had tagged along with my cousin to our family lake house."

I couldn't tell if I was coming off as casual as I hoped or if I was clearly trying too hard and failing. It seemed like the proper amount of details, but really I was no good judge of anything just then.

"That's so romantic. So they were childhood sweethearts?"

I shook my head. "Wrong cousin. He came along with Savannah's older brother. According to her, Emerson only recently took an interest in her. Makes sense though. I mean, there's about eight years between them." Ten between us.

Steph shrugged. "Still sweet."

"I guess. If you're into that gag-me sort of sweetness." I felt myself make a face and instantly regretted it. Way to act like a grown up.

I could see Steph studying me out of the corner of my eye, but she dropped the topic all together and moved onto something else.

"So, let's see this dress you've been working on." She was already up on her feet and headed for the door as if she knew exactly where she was going. I'd been in the house for almost two days now and I never walked three feet in any direction around here with that kind of confidence.

"Um, there's not much of a dress yet. Just a design and a few bags of fabric." I was slowly catching up to her at the door.

"What's our sewing situation?"

"You mean in terms of machines? Well, there's my Noonie Skeeter's old one, but it's from the early 1900's so I don't plan on using it," I said dryly as I led the way to my room.

"So we're doing the whole job by hand?" I could tell I had scared her a little.

"No. They didn't have the one I wanted in stock when we went shopping yesterday, so they had to bring it down from another store. Should be there this evening. Savannah said she'd swing by there after work to grab it and bring it here so I can get started. But that's only going to go so far…"

Once inside, I went over to the desk beneath the window to retrieve the sketch. I handed it to Stephanie.

"Beading?!" she shouted as she fell back into the chair behind her.

As dresses went, Savannah's beading was actually quite minimal. This had been intentional of course knowing that the dress had to be done in less than two weeks and that I would be the only one around to make that happen. Of course, even with that knowledge at the forefront of my mind, I had gotten slightly carried away during the design process and we would now have to suffer the consequences of my ambitions.

"I'm sorry! I was having a creative moment. Besides, I was planning on doing it all myself anyway, so don't even worry about it. You can work on the other stuff using the machine. I swear."

Stephanie twisted her mouth at me, still visibly dissatisfied with my poor judgment. "Well, it *is* a really pretty dress."

"Thank you."

"So, I guess we should get started cutting the fabric and pinning the dress together?"

I nodded. "Just as soon as we find a place to do that."

For the amount of material involved, we were going to need a very large work surface. The only place that came to mind was sitting in the formal dining room downstairs.

"We can try the big dinner table in the front hall."

"No time like the present." She jumped to her feet and went to start piling up the bags of material and supplies. "Let's do this." She looked like a woman on a mission. In all reality I had had no fucking clue how we were going to pull this off, but seeing her and the determination on her face was enough to make me think we could somehow manage to produce a fab wedding dress even without the proper set up or a reasonable amount of time to do it in. Even if we had to pull it out of our asses. This dress was going down.

Three hours and a hundred or so needle pricks later and we had managed to pin the dress onto the mannequin. Well, the basic shape of it anyway. There were several layers still to come.

"I need a break." I slid myself into one of the dining room chairs. "My fingers hurt. That last needle actually drew blood. If Savannah doesn't show up here soon with that sewing machine, we're not going to get much further than this today."

While I was having a marvelous whine to myself, Stephanie had taken to pacing. She was tapping the side of her chin with her pen as she went. An odd habit if you ask me, but it seemed to help her think so I never questioned it. Although, I'd been tempted to plenty of times. Especially when I'd seen the ink marks it left behind.

I was about to continue on with a healthy pathetic sob, when I heard the glass doors to Noonie's old hutch open.

"Hey. I've seen this place before. What is it?" Stephanie was already closing the space between us, her hand outstretched and waving around a picture frame.

"Um, you're going to have to stop doing that if you want me to actually see what you're talking about." I reached out and placed my hand on her wrist to steady it. "Oh, that's the lake house," I answered matter-of-factly. "How do you know about it?"

"Hang on." Next thing I knew, Stephanie was running from the room. A moment later I heard footsteps moving rapidly over the stairs and my confusion only mounted. Then, I heard the entire show backwards as she made her way toward me again.

"Here." She handed me a large flat package.

"What is it?"

"It's Savannah's collage. Check it out."

I ripped open the end and slid the board out carefully to have a look.

"Oh." Right there in the center of it all was a blown up picture of the lake house. "My mother's planning on moving the wedding to Lake Kentucky?"

"I guess. How far is it?"

"Four hours. And that's if the traffic is decent. Actually, if that's where she's throwing the wedding maybe we should just go ahead and get started without her. We could go out there and check it out. I'll talk to Noonie Skeeter and see about setting something up. Who knows, at this rate, we may just stay through the weekend and work from there. Might make more sense anyway. Plus, there'd be less distractions." I was rambling and no longer paying attention to what Stephanie was doing. In hindsight, not a great move on my part.

"You mean distractions like Emerson?"

Just like that, she had my undivided attention again. "What now?"

"This is the two of you when you were kids, isn't it?" She was holding up a second picture frame. Apparently it had been buried somewhere in the hutch along with the other one from the lake house.

I took a step toward her to get a better look. It *was* Emerson and I. The two of us had been reading. He was laying on his stomach while I had been comfortably stretched out on his back as if it was a lounge chair. I had no idea this picture had even been taken, but I remembered that afternoon perfectly.

"Yeah, that's us." I took the frame from her hand and went to put it back into the hutch. No need to waste any time taking useless trips down memory lane. That guy, he had been MY Emerson. But the guy outside riding around on his damn horse looking like a country music sex god, he was Savannah's. And the less I was confronted with things that suggested otherwise, the better off we'd all be.

"That has got to be the most darling thing I've ever seen. I'm serious. How freaking adorable were you two?"

"I'm sorry, did you just use the word darling? How old are you?" I slammed the door on the hutch ever so slightly. Then, I flinched at the sound. Way to follow through.

Stephanie came to stand in front of me, arms crossed over her chest. I could tell I was in for a lecture.

"Cal, I've been working for you for nearly two years now and we've been going non-stop with wedding after wedding since the day I started. Which means, I've gotten as close to a live-in lover as you are probably ever going to get. I know how you take your coffee. I know what to order for you off of any take-out menu. I know when you get your period because our cycles have now matched up and I even know what side of the goddamn bed you sleep on. I know all of your likes and dislikes, my friend, and you *likes* Emerson."

I threw both my hands up at her in frustration. "Where are you getting all of this? Some stupid picture that was taken a gazillion years ago?"

Steph smirked. "No. I got it from the way you first said his name, *Emerson*, like it was a dessert or something. And the way you kept stealing glances up at him the entire drive up to the house even though you were clearly forcing yourself to look the other way. Add the light in your eyes when you saw the picture just now which, by the way, turned burning red half a second later, and I'm getting a pretty clear visual of the situation." She tilted her head to the side, leaning her gaze and forcing me to look her in the eye. "Of course, the fact that you haven't actually denied it isn't hurting my theory either."

I pressed my lips together stubbornly, trying to thwart the inevitable. I didn't even last three seconds. "Fine. If you must know, I used to have a little crush on Emerson." I could feel the heat rushing to my cheeks and I had no idea if it stemmed from fury over having been bullied into making such an admission or simply humiliation. It was probably the latter.

Steph raised her brow at me. "Used to?"

"Um, yeah. For wedding planning purposes, I think it would be best if we stick with that terminology."

"Whatever you say, boss." She shook her head, quietly laughing at me. I'm not sure why she was holding back at this point. Wasn't like I couldn't hear her snickering away.

"Oh, now I'm the boss again? A minute ago you were my live-in lover."

"It's not a healthy relationship, but it works for us."

"Ain't that the truth?! Well, lover, I'm going to go track down my grandmother. Want to get started on packing up all this crap so we can move it back upstairs? Even if Savannah does show up here tonight with that sewing machine, I sure as hell don't plan on using it anymore."

Steph was already moving in the direction of our mannequin. "I'm on it."

"That's why you're my person." I pointed at her dramatically as I backed out of the room and left to search for Noonie Skeeter.

I spent longer than necessary hanging around the property that night. I'd hoped my paths would cross with Lissy's at some point during the day, but it hadn't worked out that way. After the way she had acted the night before, I couldn't help but wonder if she was avoiding me on purpose.

"You takin' off or stayin'?" It was Burke.

I looked down at Reesie sitting at my feet. "Depends. Which do you want me to do?"

He smirked, handed me a blanket and full cup of coffee and said, "You're stayin'. Majestic's lookin' like tonight may be the night. Was just headed to her stall myself, but I'd just as soon have you spend the night here. My pillow top mattress is better on my joints than the bedding in her stall."

I nodded. "Have a good night."

I watched as the old man bent down to pat my dog and then walked out giving me a backwards wave. "And thanks for the coffee." Finally I'd have an excuse to go up to the house. Pattie'd have some sort of sweet pastry sitting up in the kitchen which was bound to partner well with coffee.

The house was quiet when I walked in through the front door. No one ever locked the place up. Which I suppose would seem strange to outsiders, seeing a place like this, knowing the kind of wealth that filled it and then finding out nobody was doing anything to secure it. Well, that wasn't entirely true. Troy Ashcraft was rumored to sleep with a shotgun under the bed and I'd seen Skeeter in action with a bullwhip. Anytime I heard the expression "looks can be deceiving" those two were always the first thing that came to mind. They had to be in their eighties by now and aside from Troy's enormous size and natural lack of smile and the scary alert look in Skeeter's eyes, the pair wasn't exactly intimidating. But knowing what I knew about the Ashcraft patriarchs, I'd be the first to tell you not to cross them. Hell, maybe I'd tell you to go for it just so I could see you get your ass whupped.

Of course neither were near as terrifying as Pattie, who'd likely come after me with her cast iron skillet if she walked in and caught me stealing a healthy portion of her peach cobbler.

With a mounded plate in my hand, I stood out in the dark foyer for a moment contemplating my options. I had hoped for a possible run-in with Lissy, but aside from the low hum of chatter coming from upstairs there was no sign of her. I half considered going up there and knocking on her door, but it was already after nine and just showing up at her bedroom without an invitation might not have gone over well. So I left again, as undetected as I'd entered.

As I walked back to the barn and had my seat on a stack of hay bales in the aisle across from Majestic's stall, I tried to sort it all out for myself. In a way, being with Liss was completely comfortable. I knew her. She knew me. Maybe I hadn't seen her in two decades, but when we had spent time together, she'd been around non-stop for three months and I'd had no choice but to get used to sharing my space with her. Only now things were a little bit different.

I still felt like it was perfectly normal to reach out and take her hand, or wrap my arm around her, only she was probably far less likely to beg me for a piggy back ride when she got tired or try and climb up onto my shoulders when she wanted a better point of view. Still, she felt like Lissy. Just a new, updated version.

She was a woman now. A woman who had all of the best parts of the little girl who had made me laugh over and over again. Who had taught me about patience. Had made me understand the responsibility I had to look out for those more vulnerable than myself. Even at six, she had challenged me, had pushed me to be better without even knowing it, simply because she needed me to be, and I had grown up to be a better man because of her. Except I'd never even realized it until that very moment when I was sitting alone in the dark waiting for Majestic's foal to arrive.

Five hours later and there was still no change. I was starting wonder if tonight was really going to be the night. Either way, if I was going to stay awake any longer, I was going to need another cup of coffee.

I left Reesie to watch over the laboring mare while I went to get a refill from the coffee pot in Burke's office. Not surprisingly, it was cold and iced lattes weren't my thing. So, my mug filled, I headed back over to the main house to pop it into the microwave.

Considering it was now after one o'clock in the morning, I had no false hopes this time of crossing paths with Lissy. Which is why she scared the shit out of me when I nearly ran into her walking out of the kitchen in the dark.

"Holy shit, Liss," I hissed, now wearing half of my coffee. "Why don't you turn on a light?"

"Why don't you?" she shot back, looking slighted. "What are you doing sneaking around here in the middle of the night anyway? I thought you had a place off property."

"I do," I could hear myself sounding indignant as well, as if she'd just accused me of robbing the place blind or something. "We've got a mare about to foal. I'm on night duty." I peered down at my clinging wet shirt, "And not that it matters now, but my coffee was cold and needed a reheat."

She had to squint in the dark to see what I was talking about. "Oh. Sorry." Then, "Wait, did you say one of the horses is about to have a baby?"

"Uh-huh." An unexpected opening and I'd be damned if I didn't jump on it. "You wanna come see?"

Even without any light I could tell she was smiling.

"Seriously? That would be amazing."

"Alright then." I nodded, trying hard to contain my enthusiasm. "Go put on some boots and let's go."

A few minutes later, we were outside, making our way down to the barn.

"Oh shit." I heard a scuffle behind me and caught her arm just as she was tumbling down.

"You okay?"

She was straightening herself out again already. "Yeah, just tripped."

"Sorry, I should have warned you. The walkway is pretty uneven. Guess I'm just used to it." I slid my hand down her arm until my fingers anchored in hers. She didn't say a word, just pressed her palm to mine and kept walking while I led the way.

Once inside, we quietly headed toward the back. I could hear Majestic groan. Things were progressing faster than I'd thought.

"Stay right here," I whispered when we reached the spot in the aisle where Reesie was still sitting exactly the way I'd left her. Then I opened the stall door, and slowly crept in along the side of the wall so I'd be close enough to assist Majestic if she needed me to.

She was already lying on her side and the foals hooves had begun to pass. If all went as it was supposed to the baby's head would be out shortly.

Majestic was breathing heavily, stretching and shifting her weight around in her effort to best position herself to push. After a few more sessions, the head was free. Majestic and I had been through several births together already. She was a pro and most times, I was merely there for moral support. While she rested up in preparation of the hardest part, the shoulders and hips, I slowly reached over and gently removed the smooth, thin, white sac still covering the foal's head. Then, taking a strand of straw, I tickled its muzzle, ensuring the foal was alert and breathing.

From then on, I sat back and watched as Majestic performed a perfect birth all on her own. Soon, mother and child were both resting side by side, worn out from the excitement of the night's events, but both strong and healthy.

Careful not to disturb them, I gingerly made my way back out into the barn aisle, where Liss was still standing, eyes glistening and smiling from ear to ear. I knew exactly how she'd felt. Didn't matter how many times I saw it, few things in life could compare to the lengths a mother would go to for her child, starting with bringing it into the world safely.

We stood there, neither of us saying anything. Just watching. Then, when the colt began to stir, I felt her hand grip my arm just above my wrist, squeezing it tighter as she watched in anticipation while the foal stood for the very first time.

I could have stayed there with her all night. Not talking. Just being. It would have been more than enough for me. But, I knew she wasn't here to keep me company. She wasn't here for me at all. She was here for the wedding.

"I better get you back up to the house." I nudged her gently in the side and she began to walk toward the barn doors again.

Once we stepped outside, she paused, and then, out of nowhere, flung both arms around my neck, pressing her body to mine in the process. I was so stunned, I froze.

"Thank you." Her breath tickled my ear as she whispered. "Just, thank you."

Then, as I was coming to my senses and about to return the gesture, she released me and hurried out into the darkness toward the house.

Chapter 7

With no sign of my mother and a simple three word text notifying me that she would 'be there Friday', Steph and I took off in Noonie Skeeter's truck and headed out to the lake house. Considering Savannah hadn't showed up with the new sewing machine until after nine p.m. the night before, Stephanie and I had taken the night off and spent it lounging on the bed watching a Sex In The City marathon and stuffing our faces with Pattie's homemade peach cobbler à la mode.

Shortly after Steph had gone to bed, I had ventured back downstairs for a glass of water to dilute all of the sugar still surging through my system. That was when I had run into Emerson. Naturally, I decided to omit my late night outing to the barn when I saw Steph the next morning, but I was still thinking about Emerson as well as Pattie's sweet peaches as I was making the best out of my limited driving skills headed toward the lake house.

"Do you have any idea what you're doing over there?" Steph asked after I spent five minutes checking my mirrors before actually taking the plunge and changing lanes on a highway riddled with cars all desperate to get around me.

"Yes!" It came out automatically. Honesty took a second longer. "No!"

"Yeah, well it shows," she grumbled as she double checked her seatbelt to make sure it was fitted nice and snug.

"Hey, I offered you the driver's seat and you refused," I retorted.

"I don't have a fucking license," she gasped. "I've lived in Manhattan my entire life. No one I know actually has their own car, except *your* family."

"Yeah, well, my mother might have a car, but it comes with a fucking driver! Not like I've had a lot of chances to practice either." The more I talked about it, the more I began to panic. This had been a bad idea. Why had I been so determined to make the drive myself?

"If you had just let Emerson give us a ride like your grandmother offered, we'd probably be halfway there by now."

Oh right. We were better off with my driving. Well, at least I was.

"Listen to me. I am going to get us there just like I said I would. It's not like I've *never* driven. I'm just a little rusty."

Stephanie squinted her eyes at me. "How rusty?"

I let my hand teeter in midair. "Eh....rusty like I haven't driven since Burke the barn manager let me do figure eights in the back pasture last time I was there."

"And when was that?"

"Um, about nine years ago."

"Fan-fucking-tastic. Well, I hope you're happy now, because we're both going to die, all because you were too afraid to sit in the car with secret lover cowboy."

"Okay – A, we are NOT calling him that and B, nobody is going to die." I could tell Steph was about to counter and I lifted my hand to stop her. Then, in blissed silence, I drove on.

Nearly six and a half hours later, we finally arrived at the lake house. Given our tremendous delay, the caretaker had had ample time to go through and open up the place after receiving Noonie Skeeter's call first thing that morning informing him of our impromptu visit.

In fact, by the time we pulled up, he had already left.

"Whoa." Steph was barely out of the truck and doing a complete 360 in the driveway trying to take it all in.

"I know. I felt the same way when I first saw it. Actually, I still do." It was exactly the way I'd remembered it. Part of me had been worried that like so many things, the once childish perception would prove to be somewhat distorted and exaggerated, but that was not the case. If anything, it was grander, more magnificent than I had originally viewed it.

"Forget Savannah. *I* want to get married here."

I smirked. "Get yourself a groom and I'll make it happen."

Steph cocked her head to the side to glare at me over the hood of the truck. "Get yourself a *real* live-in lover and maybe I'll have time to."

I shrugged. "Guess we're both staying single."

Eager to get inside and see if anything had changed since the last time I'd been there, I hurried for the front porch, skipping a step or so every few feet. Judging from the sound of gravel moving under rubber soles behind me, Steph was following right along.

When we reached the porch, I heard two loud sighs. It took me a second to realize, one had been from me. Something about the sight of rocking chairs just did that to you. Sigh. Yup, I did it again.

Then, with the excitement continually building, I reached for both handles on the set of all-glass French doors and pulled them open in one swift move, revealing the stunning foyer and massive wooden stair banister I had slid down once upon a time.

"Oh my God! Why doesn't anyone LIVE here? Because I will. Seriously, tell Noonie Skeeter to get rid of the groundskeeper. I'm taking over." Steph was slowly walking through the room, shaking her head in awe with each step she took.

"It's amazing, isn't it? And it's exactly the way I remember it. From what I can tell, not a single thing has changed." I inhaled deeply, taking in the scent of wood and fresh water. "It even smells the same."

"How many cousins did you say you had?" Steph's eyes were closed as she stood halfway between the foyer and formal living room, just breathing in the rustic air.

"Fifteen. Why?"

She turned back to me, grinning mischievously. "Just exploring my options. I'm getting into this house one way or another."

I laughed. "Help yourself to any available Ashcrafts you like. It'd be kinda fun actually. We could be the Ashcraft Family Outcasts together."

"No way. They're all gonna love me. You're on your own with the outcast business. It's okay though, I'll still invite you to stuff. And of course, you'll get the annual Christmas card."

"Gee, thanks." It was right around then that I realized, I hadn't ever received one of those from any Ashcraft. Not that I'd ever sent any out. But that went across the board. No one ever got a card from me. Somehow I suspected this 'no card' rule didn't apply to everyone.

Once we'd managed to get our fill of woodsy scents, we finally made it through the entire house and eventually settled on two bedrooms located on the main floor, closest to all the amenities we intended to enjoy during our stay. Namely, the pool out back and the rocking chairs out front.

Given the gorgeous weather, we opted for the pool first.

Of course we had way too much work to do to go swimming, but that didn't mean we couldn't work on our tans while diving into non-stop dressmaking mode. Utilizing an outdoor extension cord and multiple large patio tables, we created a massive work station suitable for our needs.

Since Pattie had been kind enough to pack us a picnic for the drive, we hadn't yet had to make time for meals. Between pulled pork sandwiches, fresh potato salad, homemade lemonade and to die for brownies, Steph and I had been eating our way through the day quite happily. But, as the evening began to creep up on us, thoughts of dinner began to swirl about in my head, slowly but surely taking over until the need for food became so overwhelming there was no focusing on anything else anymore.

It was just as well. We had already achieved as much as we were going to for the day. The only thing I definitely needed to get started on after we ate was the beading on the dress. With everything that had happened in the last forty-eight hours, I'd been happy to put it off, but considering how fast the wedding date was creeping up on us, that really was no longer an option.

"Any thoughts on food?" Steph was wandering around the large kitchen opening and closing drawers trying to get a feel for things.

"Yes. Lots." I went straight for the fridge. "Alright. Now we're talking." Apparently the caretaker had done more than just open the blinds and set up the pool. The fridge was stocked from top to bottom in everything you could possibly want. The freezer was more of the same.

"Holy shit. Check out this pantry." Steph was standing in the doorway to what could easily have been mistaken for an additional bedroom had it not been for the fact that the walls were lined from floor to ceiling with massive shelves containing enough food to stock a small grocery store. "Well, at least we won't have any reason to do any more driving anytime soon."

"Always a plus." I was crunching away on a carrot. The veggie platter sitting front and center of the fridge had been too tempting to pass by. "Care to dip?"

"Yes, please." Steph went straight for the mini bell peppers.

From there we just sort of started pulling random items to the kitchen table and continued our grazing until we moved on to sweeter items like cookies and ice cream, at which point I no longer considered it grazing. It was more like heifering.

I was just in the middle of sliding half of a chocolate chip cookie through the carton of peanut butter cup ice cream when my phone exploded in the sounds of ABBA belting Dancing Queen, a clear classic if you ask me.

"What's up, Tor?"

"I'm really, really sorry."

I crinkled my brow, already frowning. "About what?" Whatever it was, it couldn't be good. Tori made it a habit to rarely apologize for anything.

"Oh, you don't know yet?" It was half statement, half question.

"Don't know what? Could you please just come out and say whatever it is you need to say?" I hated surprises. Especially ones that started with 'I'm sorry.'

Tori still hadn't answered me when I heard Steph pipe up from across the kitchen.

"Um, I think your boyfriend's here." Shit was seriously getting confusing.

I dashed for the window she was peering out of and spotted Reesie running toward the house. I spun back around to scold Steph. "How many times do I have to say that he is *not* my boyfriend?"

Then, *click*, I heard the line go dead and Tori had removed herself from the conversation all together. It was just as well. Her surprise would have to wait until after I figured out what the hell Emerson was suddenly doing here.

I marched straight to the front door and yanked it open, all the while ignoring Steph's continued muttering behind me as she followed along. I was barely to the edge of the porch when I stopped dead in my tracks.

"Tyler?"

"Surprise!"

I was way too stunned to speak, let alone do anything to stop him as he practically ran over to me and wrapped me in his arms as if I'd been yearning to be held by them for an eternity. Truth was, neither Tyler nor his muscly arms and torso had even crossed my mind since before I left town.

When I saw his lips zeroing in on mine, I finally managed to make a move. Even if it was just to turn my head to dodge what, based on his embrace, would likely have been an overzealous kiss.

"Babe, you have no idea how much I've missed you." Tyler was busy running his fingers through my thick hair and pulling it back to get a better look at my face. Honestly, I'm a little shocked he didn't reverse his actions the second he saw my expression, which was certainly less than thrilled.

I thought I heard a hissing sound and turned just in time to see Emerson's back as he disappeared inside the house without so much as a hello. As tempting as it was to try and analyze Emerson's odd behavior, I simply didn't have the time. Not with Tyler's lips coming at me yet again, this time parted. I swear I saw some tongue tip creeping out just before I ducked and slipped out of his clutches.

"Tyler, what are you doing here?" I demanded. The shock of it all was wearing off and quickly morphing into anger.

"Look, I thought about what happened the other day –"

"You mean the part where we broke up?"

He closed in on me yet again, this time placing both of his hands on my shoulders and leaning into me from up on his six foot three frame. "Baby, no one breaks up over having to share a shower."

"Actually, they do. We did, in fact." How was he not getting this? And more importantly, how could I make it any clearer?

"Don't be silly, Callie. We're perfect for each other and you know it. You just need a little more time to get over being so overly independent and you'll see what a great couple we make." I didn't know what was grinding my last nerve more. The fact that he insisted on calling me Callie – a nickname I hated, or the fact that he was being a condescending asshole while doing it.

"See that's the thing though, Tylie. I don't plan on getting over my annoying over- independence. It's just who I am. And, I'm okay with that. Since you're not, I'm thinking maybe we're not as great a couple as you've led yourself to believe." I gave him a pat on the back as I walked past him and returned to the front porch. I only hoped I came across as patronizing as he had a moment ago.

"You can't be serious."

I stopped and turned back. "Why not?"

"I came all the way out here to see you. I brought a ring for fuck's sake!" He was getting pissed.

"You really should have called first." I spun around on my heel and headed straight for the front door. Without looking back I called out, "You can stay here for the night. Just pick a room somewhere where I won't have to see you and we'll be good. You can arrange for a ride out of here first thing in the morning."

If he said anything else in response, I was too far away to hear it.

It wasn't until I was back inside and heard voices coming from the kitchen that I realized Steph had left me to fend for myself out there somewhere along the way.

"That was interesting," she said dryly when I walked in.

"Couldn't really have thought so since you didn't stick around to watch it play out." Sometimes I probably took her responsibilities as my assistant to the extremes. It probably wasn't part of her job to hold my hand during a run in with a clingy, somewhat thick-headed ex. Still felt like it should have been though.

"You can tell me all about it in the morning. After the drive up here, I've had my share of near death experiences for one day."

I watched as she placed our empty plates in the sink. "How would my telling you about Tyler's visit be a near death experience?"

"Oh, it would be a death of boredom." She grinned at me. "Anyway, I'm going to bed." If she hadn't given a sly sideways glance in Emerson's direction, I might have taken her little dig personally. As it was, her motives for ditching me for the second time in less than five minutes while in the company of a man I was less than thrilled about, were clear as glass.

The moment Stephanie was gone, I swear I felt a chill cast over the room. Even from the doorway I could feel Emerson's whole demeanor change.

"How'd you get roped into this whole mess?" It was the only thing I could think of even if the answer would likely trace back to my grandmother.

"He showed up at the farm looking for you. Noonie asked me to bring him out. So, I did." He tipped back the beer he was holding and took a long sip.

"Noonie, huh? Guess you already think you're family." God, why was I being such a bitch to this man?

Emerson's bottle hit the counter with a loud clank. "I'm sorry. You have a problem with me calling Skeeter Noonie? Why? It doesn't count since I'm not related by blood?"

"No, marriage will work just fine. I'm just saying, maybe wait until after you make that trip down the altar."

"Just who the hell is it I'm supposed to be marrying? I know planning weddings is kind of your thing, but maybe you could stick to planning ones for people who ask you to." He hadn't raised his voice any, but there was definitely an edge to his tone I hadn't ever heard before. Like a quiet fury just simmering below the surface, controlled but raw.

"Are you fucking kidding me right now? I was *asked* to plan your wedding! You really think coming here on a moment's notice to throw all this shit together was *my* idea?!" I on the other hand was shouting. Nothing controlled about what was bubbling below, or rather spilling over.

Emerson's mouth half opened and then immediately shut again. For a moment, I thought I had him. Thought I'd won. Then, I saw the sides of his mouth begin to twitch and the corners of his eyes crinkled. I'd seen it happen often enough to know he was about to laugh at me. "You think I'm marrying Savannah." There was no question about it.

"Well, yeah!" I replied indignantly. "Wait. Aren't you?"

"Hell no, I'm not marryin' her! Are you kidding me? We'd kill each other before the honeymoon was over. Besides, she's Spence's little sister, which makes her like *my* sister."

Stunned, I was too beside myself to put it all together on my own. "But she said she was marrying her brother's best friend. That's YOU!"

Emerson was still grinning. "You really need to come out for more family reunions, Liss. Spence ain't Savannah's only brother. There's the oldest, Simon, as well."

I have no idea how long I stood there like a fucking statue, my arms up in the air and mouth wide open. It seemed like an eternity before I finally managed to speak again. And even then, it wasn't much.

"Oh."

"Yeah, oh. Don't you think I might have mentioned I was the groom when we were hanging out the other day? Or any time after? I mean, I think that sort of stuff is worth mentioning. Even if some people don't."

I noticed the smile fading from his eyes, in spite of the fact that he was making every effort to keep his lips drawn up.

"Well, I'm glad to hear that." Maybe now that all of that was cleared up we could move on to less awkward territory.

"While we're on that, was there anything you wanted to share?" He was cocking his head to the side and giving me a probing glare, as if he was daring me to deny something. Only I had no idea what I was supposed to confess.

"Not particularly, no." Increasingly uncomfortable from the way his eyes were boring into me, I busied myself with putting away the last of our buffet of snacks.

"Just as well I guess. Your boyfriend already gave me an earful on the drive up here."

I snorted. "Yeah, I bet he did. Of course, it probably wasn't anything compared to what he'll have to say tomorrow on his ride back out of here."

I turned back from the pantry and caught a glimpse of Emerson out of the corner of my eye. The smile from before was gone now and had been replaced with a turned in lower lip which was apparently being gnawed on. I assumed it was his version of Steph's thoughtful pen tap since he had remained strangely silent. An uncomfortable move mid-conversation and I hated having been the last one to say something. How long did I wait to speak again? Did I speak again? Maybe it was time to just wave and walk out of the room.

I was mid contemplation myself, twisting my left index and middle finger in my right hand – because that was *my* thing, when Emerson said, "I'm starting to think we have some serious communication issues, which is ironic really because the other day...well, never mind that now. You're not together with that guy anymore, are you?"

"No. We broke up last week. I have no idea what possessed him to come up here out of the blue." Then, to make sure he knew it was really done with I added, "Because it was over for me way before that already. I just didn't know how to tell him...or anyone else."

His entire energy shifted as he leaned back against the counter behind him, completely losing that foreboding thing he'd had going on a minute earlier when he was getting on my case about how annoying Tyler had been. "Who else would you need to tell?"

I sighed. "My mother and my friend Tori. Not that either of them were all that surprised. But, that's pretty much the reason I was dreading it. They have this not so secret fear that I will end up alone like a crazy old cat lady. Which is stupid, because I'm allergic to cats, so that's obviously not happening." Why was I still talking?

If nothing else, my embarrassing rambling was bringing the smile back to Emerson's eyes. Even if it was at my expense, I felt a rush of butterflies storm through the pit of my stomach knowing I had put it there.

"I seriously doubt you'll end up alone, Liss. Crazy maybe, but not alone." There was something sweet about his tone and I chose to ignore the part where he was clearly making fun of me.

"I'm really sorry you got stuck having to bring Tyler all the way out here. I'm sure you had better things to do today. Not to mention, carting around your boss's granddaughter's ex-boyfriend probably isn't part of the job description."

He chuckled. "I didn't mind. Well, I mind less now that I know you're not still with him."

His tone went soft and the contours of his face changed, revealing the boy still hiding within the man.

"Why would you care if I was with him or not?" I could feel my insides vibrate with anticipation as I waited for his answer. I don't know what I thought I was going to hear. A grand confession of love after one measly afternoon of fishing and sightseeing, if you could even call it that since we never left the property. Still, part of me was unable to detach from the six year old romantic who had felt it was so obvious that we'd live happily ever after one day.

But he simply shrugged and said, "You could do better." Then he gave a little whistle to Reesie signaling their exit and began to move past me to leave.

The rhythm of nerves that had set my body abuzz, dropped into my gut like a solid rock and suddenly I felt ridiculous for assuming that Emerson's annoyance with Tyler was anything more than just due to his obnoxious personality. After all, it had annoyed me plenty during the year we'd dated.

"That's really none of your business though, is it?!" I snapped as Emerson walked out of the kitchen. He paused in the doorway a moment before turning around.

"You're right, it's none of my business. Sorry. It's just…"

"What?"

"When I think of you, I'm always going to remember that little girl who grabbed my hand in the woods when she got scared, or expected me to catch her if she slid while climbing on the rocks when we were fishing down by the lake. I know we haven't seen each other in almost twenty years, but having you here again, it doesn't feel any different. Whether it's from falling on a slippery rock or some undeserving asshole who isn't worth your time, I'm always going to want to protect you, Lissy."

He smiled, but there was a strange sadness about him and suddenly I had an overwhelming urge to run toward him and wrap my arms tightly around his neck. I didn't, but I definitely wanted to.

"I get it. It doesn't feel any different for me either."

I automatically walked the length of the house until I reached the game room off of the garage. Right below was the basement which was where Spence and I had stayed every time we came up here.

As expected, I still had clothes in the dresser from the last time we'd come out to do some fishing. It had been several years, but there was no reason they wouldn't still fit.

I grabbed a towel from the linen closet and headed for the shower. After, I searched the medicine cabinet and found everything I needed from deodorant to a toothbrush. Noonie Skeeter always had the place stocked better than a five star hotel.

Then, with nothing left to do, I threw myself back into the bed which Reesie was already happily occupying and reached for the remote. I must have flipped through every channel at least three times before I settled on the Food Network. Wasn't like I was really going to watch anything anyway. Mostly I just wanted something to drown out the noise of my own thoughts.

Coming out here had been a bad idea. Shit was getting more and more confusing by the minute. First Liss and I had that magic moment in the barn and I thought for one stupid second that something was happening between us only to be introduced to her 'fiancé' a few short hours later.

Of course Noonie Skeeter had volunteered me to give him a ride up here, but the truth was I'd have probably nominated myself for the job anyway. A sick curiosity had taken over the second Tyler had shown up asking for 'Callie'. At first I'd thought he'd landed at the wrong farm. No one there had ever called her that. Sure, I seemed to be the only one still calling her Lissy or Liss, but from what I'd gathered she was now going by Calista or Cal. Definitely *not* Callie. She wasn't a Callie.

On the upside, my instincts about Tyler the dipshit had been dead on. And, even better, he was already history. Except now I was wondering if maybe I was too.

Seeing that little punk, realizing that this was the sort of guy she'd been dating, made me realize several things. For starters, I was old. Not Santa Claus old, but old enough. At twenty-three I'd thought thirty-three sounded like a million years away and for all I knew, Lissy was looking at me and thinking the exact same thing.

Then there was the issue of style. Tyler had the look. He fit the part. Seeing her stand beside him, it made sense. Even in her sweet summer dress and cowboy boots, she'd never look like she belonged to me. No matter how much my heart was already telling me she did.

Chapter 8

It was nearly midnight when my phone rang. I had completely lost track of time working on Savannah's gown and the sound of 'Hillbilly Bone' cutting through the silence scared the crap out of me.

"Noonie? What's wrong?"

"Why would anything be wrong?"

I glanced at the time twice to make sure I'd read it right in my hurry to answer the phone. I had. "Because it's the middle of the night, Noonie. Shouldn't you be sleeping or something?"

"What are you, my mother?! I don't have no damn bedtime."

I stifled a laugh. "My bad. Okay then, what's up?"

"Nothin' much. Just wonderin' if I should be expectin' a double weddin' here next Sunday."

Fucking Tyler. He'd told my grandmother? He didn't even know her.

"No, Noonie. No double wedding. Not now. Probably not ever. And for the record, if any unheard of boyfriends ever show up to surprise me in the future, feel free to send your boot up their asses and kick them back to where they came from."

I could hear her chuckle on the other end. "I'll be sure to make a note of that for next time, darlin'. In the meantime, I trust you had your mother's old boots on hand to do the job yourself?"

I looked down at my feet. I did actually. For some strange reason I'd been wearing them non-stop since I'd found them up in her old closet. They were hardly my style, and yet I was going out of my way to make them work with the wardrobe I had packed. Which wasn't easy by the way.

"Oh, they got the job done alright." I was cracking up all throughout this conversation. It made me wonder why I hadn't ever been closer to my Noonie Skeeter. Someday my mother would have to explain to me what happened back in Kentucky that made her turn her back on everyone and so rarely look back.

"I'm glad to hear it. Of course, if you had run into any snags, I'm sure Emerson would have been more than happy to help you." Something about the way she said it made me feel like she was leading into a new topic.

"Yeah, I guess he does have a way of looking out for me. Apparently it's my fault. He says I inadvertently assigned him the job when I was little."

Noonie Skeeter was quiet for a while and I wondered if old age had suddenly caught up and sent her to sleep. "If I recall correctly, you assigned him a bigger part in your heart than that, Calista."

"Noonie, I was just a child with a silly crush." Why was everyone so hell-bent on distorting something I was trying hard to keep simple.

"Just remember, Calista, neither of you may be children anymore, but nothing else has changed. You still come from different worlds, live in different places and have been brought together by circumstances which won't last."

I wasn't sure what to make of that. Maybe she was imparting a sage piece of wisdom I would have to decipher for myself in my own time. Or, maybe Noonie Skeeter wasn't as with it as she seemed.

"Alright Noonie, well I better get back to this dress if we expect to see Savannah walk down the aisle in more than just her underwear."

"Don't stay up too late now, there'll be more to do come daylight."

After she hung up, I sat there for several seconds longer with the phone still to my ear as if I was waiting for her to add some last minute token of insight, even if it was a bit abstract.

After all the confusion between Emerson and I both jumping to the wrong conclusions these last few days, and my random and more and more frequent trips down memory lane, it would have been helpful to have a voice of experience whispering the answers in my ear.

"Damn, my life just up and went all Hallmark on me." It was a sad, sad realization and I put the phone down in one determined motion. I was here for one reason and one reason only. Savannah's wedding. And, as it turned out, Emerson no longer had anything to do with that.

With an ironclad focus I returned to my sewing machine and got back to work, forcing all thoughts of Emerson from my mind. When I ran out of the will required to continue fighting it, I found solace in knowing that he would be leaving, along with Tyler, first thing in the morning.

Five hours of sewing and forty-five minutes of sleep later, I was stumbling through the house in the dark in search of the kitchen. There was no need to bother with lights, since technically my eyes weren't open anyway.

I was nearly there when I became aware of the thing leading my way. It was the heavenly scent of coffee. My heart sang for joy. *Stephanie.*

"Good morning, Lover," I chirped happily as I walked through the large arched doorway.

"Well, good morning to you, too, Beautiful." Not Stephanie. Definitely not Stephanie.

"Shit. Sorry, I thought you were Steph," I mumbled as I went back to walking with my eyes closed and my head down until I ran into the back counter housing the coffee maker.

"You call your assistant 'Lover'?" he smirked. I could barely raise my gaze to look at him. Emerson wasn't exactly clothed as he stood there barefoot and shirtless, wearing nothing but his very well worn and well fitted jeans that hung from his hips and ass perfectly. Not that I was looking. Oh hell, how could you not look?! Those tight shirts he'd been wearing hadn't told the half of it. His arms and chest were chiseled perfection. His flawless skin wasn't hurting the visual either, nor was the lack of the dreaded farmer's tan which naturally sparked images of him working shirtless on a hot summer day, doing whatever it was that kept his body in a state I would deem worthy of being labeled underwear model-like.

I took a deep breath in and exhaled loudly with no regard to the fact that I was now obviously ogling the man. Then I remembered that he had asked me something.

"I'm sorry, what did you say?" I shook my head back and forth a few times trying to jumble up the image of a half-naked Emerson I now had plastered at the forefront of my mind.

"I asked if you always call your assistant 'Lover'." His level of amusement was definitely on the rise.

"Oh, yeah. She makes me coffee. Most of the time it's better than the sex I've been having, so 'Lover' seems appropriate."

"Sounds like yet another reason to raise your standard in men," he said smugly as he lifted his mug to those gorgeous lips.

Then, for the first time since wandering into the kitchen I became aware of my own appearance when I strolled by the microwave cradling my coffee cup. My reflection nearly made me jump across the room.

I've always considered myself to be quite organized. Just maybe not in the way most people are. For example, while sewing or working on a project in general, I liked to keep things I might need on hand. I did this by pinning a lot of stuff into my hair. Hence, the messy up do I was sporting with a variety of ribbons stuck to my head via bobby pins, along with small bags of beads and a selection of thread choices I had tied into several larger chunks of hair.

In my mind it always looked like a fucking masterpiece when it was happening, but after having slept on it, not so much. Then there was the issue of my face, which had once upon a time been made up with a soft smoky eye, some liner and mascara which now had given way to two black eyes three days post the boxing match.

Naturally, my outfit left much to be desired for also. Or perhaps, lack of outfit would have been a better choice of words, since I was basically parading around the house in what was nothing more than a slip. It was comfy like you wouldn't believe, but somewhere during the night, I had gotten cold and had paired the dainty silk piece with a pair of wool boot socks pulled up to my knees. Based on the chill on my left calf, one had slipped a bit during the course of my brief nap.

It was around this time that I noticed Emerson had been staring at me fairly intently for a great deal of time and neither of us had said anything since I had chosen to compare sex to coffee.

"So how is it?" he finally asked, nodding at my cup and breaking the awkward silence that was setting in.

"Pretty good actually."

"Better than sex?"

"Don't know, haven't had any of that yet." What on earth was I doing? For someone who looked like they ought to be pushing a shopping cart along the highway, I certainly had an unusual amount of gumption. Maybe the lack of sleep was making me delirious.

Thank God Emerson laughed as if I'd made a joke. I went ahead and just went with that.

"I take it you slept at your sewing machine?" he asked, pointing at my hair and changing the topic.

"Basically. I didn't mean to. Just kind of happened." I pushed up and slid myself backwards onto the counter to have a seat, remembering to cross my legs at a slightly delayed pace.

"I thought maybe. I heard the machine stop going and then a soft thud after, when your head hit the table. Or, at least that's what I assumed it was. You plan on going back to bed for a bit then?"

"You mean this morning? No. I've got too much to do. The dress needs to be finished and ready for a first fitting by this weekend. There will be no sleeping until after this wedding is over and Savannah and her groom are off on their honeymoon."

He smirked. "His name is Justus by the way. He's an accountant. Much more Savannah's speed than say, a horse trainer."

I was about to tell him how he sounded like a stereotyping ass when we both turned our head toward the commotion coming from the foyer. Next, Tyler was shuffling into the room looking half asleep and clearly having spent the night in his clothes.

"What are you doing up this early?" I couldn't help but feel a little annoyed seeing him awake before seven a.m. when he had slept like the dead at my house, causing my constant tardiness during our relationship.

His gaze washed over me, leaving his face scrunched up in disgust at my appearance.

"I have a flight to catch." Then Emerson popped into his line of vision. "What the hell is going on in here?"

Part of me wanted to dash over to press my scantily clad body to Emerson's chest just to piss Tyler off, and of course for other reasons not worth mentioning now, but I opted for outrage instead.

"What's it to you?" I demanded as I moved down from the counter and landed back on my feet.

"We were practically engaged less than a week ago and now you're already out here banging the help?" He didn't look so sleepy anymore now that he was flying at me, throwing his hands up in anger.

Tyler didn't have time to reach his destination though because Emerson stepped directly into his path. "That's enough."

Even though Emerson was shorter than Tyler by at least three inches, and not nearly as bulky, he wasn't the one I was suddenly worried about. Watching the two of them engaged in this unexpected showdown, I was blown away by the contrast between both men. Well, really only one of them even looked like a man. Sure, Tyler had the build of a man, but he didn't carry himself like one. He was cocky and

113

arrogant, but lacked the quiet confidence Emerson exuded with such ease.

Maybe Emerson had been onto something when he said I needed to choose better men. Maybe I needed to choose men period, since clearly I'd still been dating boys.

"You need to get out of my way right now if you know what's good for you. This has nothing to do with you," Tyler snarled.

"Funny, I was just going to say the same thing to you."

"Are you two serious right now?" I stepped out from behind Emerson to try and reason with them. "This is crazy. Tyler, you have no right to be acting this way. You and I were never even close to being engaged – trust me! Even if we hadn't fought the other morning. Even if I hadn't ended it, even if you had made it around to making a proposal, I would never have said yes. I'm sorry you were more invested in the relationship than I was. I tried, but it just wasn't there for me the way it was for you."

Finally Tyler moved back. "You really think you can do better than me?"

"Any idiot can tell she could do better than you. Besides, she's young and ambitious. Getting married right now should be the last thing on her mind." Only if Emerson kept talking like that, getting married would be the *only* thing I'd be thinking about.

"I really don't think this conversation is going anywhere Tyler. We can re-hash the whole break up a million times and it's not going to change that we want different things. Emerson is right. I like my life the way is right now. And if you really cared about me, you would understand that I need to focus on myself and my career for the time being."

Tyler snorted. "That's such bullshit and you know it. This has nothing to do with your career. The reason you can't have an actual grown up relationship is because you're still stuck at fourteen hating every man, all because your daddy walked out on your mom. Well, I've got news for you, Callie. I've met your mother. She's a controlling, uptight bitch who wouldn't know the first thing about making a man happy and I'm not surprised your father took off running in the other direction. Keep doing what you're doing and you're not going to have to worry about any guy wanting you to commit. You're well on your way to turning out just like her!"

He gave me one more condescending, revolted glance and then stomped from the kitchen. Shortly after, the front door slammed. It was so loud, for a moment I thought what was left of me after Tyler's tirade would literally shatter from the noise.

I stood there completely frozen in place. Tyler had known exactly where to hit me. He had wrapped every one of my fears into one neatly packed punch and then sent it straight to my gut. I felt winded and dizzy in the aftermath. All I wanted to do was run from the room and find a place to hide, preferably somewhere so far away from the truth that I could go back to believing the lies I had told myself. Only problem was, I couldn't feel anything below my knees which made running out of the question.

"Hey. What's going on up there?" Emerson gently swiped the loose strands of hair from my forehead and tucked them back behind my ear. "You're not seriously letting what that asshole said get to you are you? Because I'll go after him right now and beat the shit out of him if you are."

115

He grinned slightly, but I could tell he was being serious.

"You don't need to beat anyone up on my account. And he was an asshole, but he was right about what he said." My hands were tingling and I tried shaking them to calm my nerves, when he reached for them and held them still in his, gently rubbing my palms with his thumbs. It worked wonders.

"How could you possibly think that?" He was standing so close to me now I could have stuck out my tongue and flicked it all over that delicious looking chest of his. Not that I was thinking about doing that.

"You wouldn't understand." I yanked my hands from his and turned away. Things were getting way too intense for comfort.

"Why not?"

"Because, Emerson. You don't have any idea who or what I've become and I have a feeling we could spend the rest of our lives getting to know one another, and you'd still never be able to see past the sweet little girl in pigtails who needed you, when you look at me." I ended my rant fully prepared to make a dramatic exit. Only I didn't get very far. Two steps in and Emerson's hand was wrapped around my wrist, pulling me back around with such force, my body didn't come to a halt again until it landed safely against his. If I had been within licking distance before, now I was close enough to take a bite.

"Well, you're wrong about at least one thing," he growled softly as he used his free hand to gently tilt my chin upward, "I sure as hell don't see a little girl in pigtails when I look at you."

He kissed me. Tentatively at first, his lips grazing mine, caressing them patiently as if he was waiting for me to catch up to the moment. It didn't take me long.

All thoughts of why this was wrong and would never work went into the ether as I wrapped both arms tightly around his neck and allowed myself to fully sink into the depths of his kiss. His grip around me tightened, pressing me to his bare chest, making me instantly wish the slip I was wearing would simply disintegrate and vanish without a trace, eliminating the only physical barrier left between us.

With the intensity mounting, my heart was beating so fast I thought it might burst.

Then –

"Good morning," Steph said casually, as if she hadn't just walked in on what had probably been the hottest moment of my entire life. "Weaning yourself off of coffee and working your way up to the real deal I see."

"I had coffee." I slowly slipped out of Emerson's arms, but his hands never left my body.

"Apparently I don't make it as well as you do," he explained.

Stephanie poured herself a cup. "Probably not sweet enough. I keep her on a constant sugar high. Anyway, probably won't need one now." She winked at me as she walked out of the room again. "Oh, if you guys are going to keep doing what you're doing you may want to move it to the shower. Your mother called and she needs us to go sample some cakes. We'll need to leave in less than an hour if you don't want to be late."

Then she was gone again.

Emerson's fingers were drumming on my hips to a silent beat I couldn't hear, but I liked the pulse of it.

117

"I guess I better go and get ready." But I made no efforts to remove myself from his hold.

"Probably ought to." Still, his hands stayed in place.

"You should probably get going, too. It's a long drive back to Lexington." My eyes were skillfully dancing around the room, perfectly avoiding his gaze.

"I'm not going anywhere."

And, for the first time since before our kiss, they were locked back onto his. "What do you mean? How long are you staying?"

"When are you heading back?"

It took me a moment to be able to think clearly enough and remember. "Monday. I have to round up the bridesmaids and take them on a last minute shopping spree."

He nodded. "Monday it is then."

"What about your job?" The last thing I wanted was for him to get in trouble on my account. But Emerson didn't seem worried.

He leaned in and kissed the tip of my nose. "It can wait."

I waited until the cab was out of sight and then walked out back to make the call.

"Hey, Noonie."

"Emerson. Why do I get the feeling I won't be seeing you today?"

I laughed. There was never getting anything past her. So, I didn't bother trying.

"Is it going to be a problem?"

"Missin' work or fallin' for my youngest grandchild?" As expected, Noonie Skeeter was already two steps ahead of me.

"Both."

"No, no problem for me. In fact," there was a sound of papers shuffling, "you'd be doin' me a favor. By stayin, I mean. The granddaughter business you'd be handlin' on your own behalf."

"Yeah, I didn't really need you to clarify that Noonie."

"I wasn't doin' it for you. I don't want to be in any way implicated in whatever has happened, is happenin' or may happen in the future between you and Calista."

She sounded strange. Concerned maybe.

"You worried people are going to start accusing you of match makin' or something?"

"Lord no, I don't match 'em even if I do tend to see who fits. Thing is, Emerson, sometimes even when two pieces go together perfectly, the rest of the puzzle doesn't always come together as well as you'd like it to."

Not much of a euphemism there. I'd spent half the night thinking of all the reasons I should have jumped into my truck by the first sign of daylight and driven away from the lake house and Lissy without ever looking back. But then I'd kissed her and all those reasons had disappeared. Now, with her removed from my arms again, the reasons were slowly coming back to me, but I was prepared to plow through each and every one of them. And if Noonie had more for me, well, I'd tackle those, too.

"I've always been good at puzzle's, Noonie. I just keep matching up the pieces one at a time. It doesn't have to be easy. Doesn't mean it won't get done eventually."

I heard the sound of paper one more time. "Good. In that case, I have some work for you to do."

Chapter 9

Steph and I were comfortably seated in the back of the cab she had insisted on calling and we were on our way to our first meeting of the day. Apparently this would be one of two different bakeries my mother had managed to scrape together and given all the excitement of my morning, I was definitely in a cake tasting kind of mood. Plus, I was freaking starving.

"And…are we going to talk about what was cooking up in the kitchen this morning?" Steph was shifting around the computer bag at her feet, attempting to get more comfortable.

"Haha, nice one." I laughed, but averted my head toward the window in hopes she wouldn't see me turn red. "There really isn't much to tell considering you caught the live show."

"Well, I still missed the opening credits. Cal, I have been through every tedious moment between you and Tyler. Have suffered through countless tales of disastrous first dates and blind set ups. No way are you holding out on me now that things are actually interesting."

I made a face. "I'm really sorry my love life has been so taxing for you. It hasn't exactly been a cake walk for me either."

"No shit. So let's talk about Emerson, who by the way, speaking of cake, bears a tasty resemblance to icing." There was a flicker of excitement in her eyes. Not the way I'd seen in Tori's every time she'd conjured up another new guy for me to meet and fall in love with. This was different.

Like she genuinely believed something significant was happening and she wanted in on it like it was a secret or something. Which, it sort of was.

I gave in. Dramatically melting into the seat cushions much like I had Emerson's embrace, I sighed loudly. "Icing. Steph, you have NO idea! This man can kiss like I've never been kissed before. I felt like I was being pulled into him by some magical force or something, like it was merging us into one. I know this sounds completely stupid. But I'm telling you, no one has ever made me feel like that before. It was like…"

Steph was leaning over the edge of her seat in anticipation. "Like what?"

"Like I belonged there. Like there was a space within his arms that only I could fill perfectly." It wasn't until then that I noticed I had been touching my lips. I dropped my hand to my lap and made a face. "It sounds completely insane, doesn't it?"

Steph just shook her head. "It sounds beautiful actually."

"Shit, Steph. What am I going to do?"

She smiled. "For now? You're just going to enjoy it."

I definitely liked the sound of that.

It was early afternoon when the cab dropped us back at the lake house and my belly flip-flopped at the sight of Emerson's truck still parked in the driveway where I'd seen it when we left.

"You didn't really think he'd be gone when we got back, did you?" Steph teased, clearly having witnessed my reaction.

"No. But I do kind of wonder what he's been doing out here all by himself all day."

My questions only multiplied when we stepped out of the cab and were greeted by what I could only imagine at that point, was the sound of a chainsaw.

"What is that?" Steph's eyes were widening.

"Some sort of power tool? Sounds like it's coming from behind the house."

Hands full of bags filled with a day's worth of cake samples and catalogs, we made a dash for the front door. I dropped my entire load in the foyer and kept going straight for the back deck. I had barely stepped one foot outside when it came into view.

"It's an arbor," I whispered.

Steph had just caught up to me. "Wait. That's like the one from the collage your mother made for Savannah. Did he build that?" Only unlike my breathy tones, she had been shouting, ensuring she would be heard over all the noise Emerson was making.

I just nodded. It covered all of the answers I had for her anyway.

Slowly, we moved toward the mini-construction zone just past the pool area. Emerson killed the saw as soon as he noticed us walking up.

"What do you think?"

"What do I think? I think it's amazing! How did you do this? And why?" Stunned I reached out to touch the elegant structure. The wood was smooth, sanded but raw and untreated.

He shrugged. "When I called Noonie Skeeter to tell her I was staying out here for a bit, she said it was just as well. Said your mom called her asking if she knew a contractor that could do a job on short notice. Noonie was going to see if Joe the caretaker wanted the gig, but since I was already here, I got it. It's been a few years since I've done anything like this, but it's turning out alright."

"Alright? It's stunning! Emerson, you have no idea what you just did for Savannah."

He reached out and hooked the loop of my trousers with his finger to snag me toward him. "Savannah's not the one I did it for, Liss."

Oh my God, he was hot. His hair was a tousled mess, just begging to have me run my hands through it and the look in his eyes as they danced over my body before meeting my own gaze was enough to make me lose my mind right then and there.

"You really shouldn't have."

His brow knitted. "Why not?"

I grinned, "Because now that my mom knows you can do this kind of stuff, the possibilities are endless and you, my friend, are going to be very busy for the next few days."

"Oooh!" Steph piped up from behind me. "Let me go get that folder of stuff that she liked but put in the maybe file!"

The slight panic on Emerson's face as he watched her run off into the house was priceless.

"Don't worry. It's just a wedding. Only the most important day in a woman's life. No pressure."

The expression on his face shifted when he realized we were suddenly alone.

"I'm not worried. Besides, if doing a little wood work means I get to spend more time here with you, I'm all for it." He was doing that tender growling thing with his deep voice and the mere sound of it sent a wave of goose bumps over my skin.

"You should probably stop doing that, Emerson," I said quietly while playing with a patch of sawdust on his white T-shirt. I could feel his ribcage contracting underneath my fingers with each breath.

He leaned into me, his chin coming down beside my temple. "Stop doing what?"

"Making me feel like I'm important. It's weird. And…I'm afraid I might get used to it."

He kissed my cheek and murmured, "That's kind of what I'm counting on."

I didn't have a chance to say anything else. Steph was back with the folder and already spreading out its contents all over one of the patio tables. "Hey Emerson, you think you could build some of these freestanding window and doorframe things? I love how they used them here to hang pictures of the groom and bride from past to present in them. Cal, I bet you could put together some fab drapery to hang around them!"

Happy for a distraction I could actually use to my advantage, I let myself get wound up in her excitement and dragged Emerson over to see what she was talking about.

"That's brilliant, Steph. Dude, between the three of us, we could take my mother's vision up to a whole new level. We might not even need her by the time she finally gets here." I was joking. Although, she deserved it considering she had more or less dumped me in Kentucky and then abandoned me until further notice. Not that I was complaining. Anymore. But it remained to be seen if she would really show up tomorrow. As of yet, I had heard nothing beyond the text she'd sent the previous morning.

Emerson tugged the page Stephanie had been referring to over to get a better idea of what we were talking about. "This? Hell yeah I could build that. It'd be easy too.

I'll need to run out for more wood though. How much more stuff like this you girls gonna need done? 'Cause I got a buddy I might call up to come out and help me."

"Yes, definitely call him!" Steph and I looked at each other and literally squealed like a bunch of twelve year olds.

"Oh my God! This is going to be awesome!" I was beside myself with giddiness. This was what it was all about. That moment you could see the big picture. The fairy tale unfolding. The perfectly orchestrated happily ever after. The best part was, I had control over my own piece of it – the dress. And yes, I realize the unhealthy implications of this minor admission. I wasn't about to be making it out loud anytime soon, so who cared?

"I think it's time we get Savannah out here." Steph handed me my phone and continued pulling out different pages displaying a wide variety of ambiance enhancing structures we would need to fulfill our new vision of the perfect Lake House Wedding and Reception.

I nodded, beamed at Emerson and walked off to make the call.

"Hey girl, how's my wedding dress comin'?"

"Oh it's coming, but that's not why I'm calling. My mom found a venue and I think it's perfect! It has everything you wanted. It's romantic and elegant with a definite country vibe about it and best of all, it's available and won't cost you a penny!" I hoped my enthusiasm would be contagious.

"Lord, please don't tell me my wedding is taking place in one of Noonie Skeeter's barns." Apparently it wasn't.

"No, no barn," I laughed. "The lake house. I'm here right now with Emerson. My mom had him build this amazing arbor which is just, well, it's like something out of a freaking wedding fantasy actually, and Steph my assistant is busy pulling together some accent pieces for him to work on. We went and sampled cake at two different bakeries out here today and they were both fabulous. I saved some samples for you, by the way." I paused when I noticed I was still the only one in love with the idea. "Look Savannah, I'll admit that when I first heard that my mother was planning on using the lake house, I thought she was doing it out of desperation. Except coming out here, seeing how it's all going to come together, honestly, if it were my wedding I would choose this over any other venue. Trust me on this, Savannah. You want the most magical moment of your life to happen right here."

There was still silence. "Savannah? If you really hate the idea, I'm sure we can still scrap it. My mom will be here tomorrow, and we all know she can work miracles when it comes to weddings –"

"No, it's not that." Her voice was all choked up like she'd been crying. Then I heard her sniff before she went on, "I've been sold on it since you said 'the lake house'. Then, listening to you talk about it and everything you guys are doing, going above and beyond to save my wedding…I just realized that having that bitch planner run out on me was the best thing that ever could have happened. What you and your mama are putting together is going to be so much more than one day of celebration, it's going to stick with me forever."

"Oh thank goodness. For a moment there I thought you were going to tell me it sucked." I laughed in a nervous 'is it safe to feel relief now' sort of way. "How soon can you come out here?"

She did a little something that sounded like slurping air up which I assumed was her attempt at regaining her composure, followed up by her standard cute girl giggle. "You said your mama was coming out tomorrow? How 'bout I catch a ride with her. Or rather, she can catch a ride with me. Think that might work?"

"I think that would be perfect. I'll call her tonight and make sure she knows to get in touch with you as soon as she lands."

"Wonderful. I can't wait to see what you're doing up there. And, thank you. Thank you so much. It really means the world to me that you would put so much effort into doing this for me."

I nodded. To myself since she couldn't see it. "You don't have to thank me at all Savannah. Truth is, I may end up getting more out of this than you do."

It was the first time I'd admitted it out loud. Even after we ended our conversation, the same sentence rang in my head over and over again. Which begged the question, what exactly was I hoping to gain? And more importantly, how badly would it hurt if I didn't get it?

While Liss went off to call Savannah, I was busy getting better acquainted with the structures I'd be building as Stephanie handed me one picture after the next.

"I never realized there was a need for freestanding barn doors at a wedding." I'd been staring at the open double doors leading to nowhere in particular for a solid minute. Part of me wanted to say no to building them on principal.

"It's a whole theme. See? We set up the doorway to signal the entrance to our wedding. We have the window and door frames filled with hanging pictures, oh, and the big wooden barrels Cal's mom ordered to use as flower stands. We put it all together and it will have this lovely, romantic, rustic, country thing happening."

I still didn't really get it, but Steph and Lissy had certainly seemed excited about it and I assumed Savannah would feel the same. So, I resigned myself to building whatever I was handed.

"You know, Cal isn't just my boss, she's also one of my closest friends." Steph looked like she was still focused on the file at her fingertips, but I was pretty sure we were about to discuss something that had nothing to with Savannah's wedding. "Cal hasn't exactly had what you might call a whole lot of success in the relationship department. She's convinced herself that she doesn't want one and that marriage is total bull, but look at what the woman does for a living. Obviously, the little girl who believes in fairy tales is still in there somewhere, no matter how hard she's tried to kill her off."

I tossed the paper I'd been holding, into my to-do pile and turned my back to the table to get a better look at Steph. "You giving me insider information?"

"Yeah, so listen up. This shit is going to make or break you. Cal is a chickenshit. She's scared of pretty much everything and because of that, she's also a total control freak. The two together make for a lethal combo when it comes to dating. Either something happens to make her rock that deer in the headlights look that makes her want to take control and cut the sucker from her life, or the sucker does something to screw up all the ducks she likes to keep so neatly in a row that she gets scared and bails. Either way, she's fucked. Personally, I blame her father, but then I blame my father, too. We all have our issues."

What she was saying was making sense. I just didn't see how exactly it was helpful. "So, you're saying…what are you saying?"

"I'm saying, learn from the Tyler's she's left in her wake. She can't be held down or chased. So you're going to have to find some other way to keep her put."

I frowned. "Any suggestions? Or is pointing out all the reasons it won't work the extent of your advice?"

"Oh, I never said it wasn't going to work. If I thought you were just another pot hole in her path, I wouldn't be wasting my breath, Emerson." She broke into a smile unexpectedly. "I saw that picture Skeeter has of the two of you. The one where she's lying on your back reading? That's the cutest stinking thing I've ever seen by the way, but more importantly it speaks volumes for her relationship with you."

"How's that?"

Steph shrugged. "Cal hates excessive contact. Super possessive about her personal space. I'm talking, like, I've seen her freak out when Tyler pulled her over to sit on his lap because he thought he was being cute or something. I heard about that shit for the next three days. And I was there when it happened, so it's not like I needed a recount of the event or anything. Anyway, her mom says she's always been that way. Even as a kid." She was giving me that look, the one with the raised brows and big eyes, like she had just made her point and was waiting for me to have my 'A-ha' moment. Only I was too busy thinking about all the times I'd crashed into Liss's personal space since she'd shown up in Kentucky a few days ago. I'd inadvertently invaded her body countless times in countless ways, starting with taking her hand to lead the way and ending with her body pressed to mine in the kitchen that morning.

"I don't think I'm getting the message here, Steph. I've been all up in her space ever since she got here."

"That's exactly my point. She's comfortable with you. She trusts you. She shares her space with you." She picked up the folders she'd been searching through and held them to her chest preparing to leave. "I'm thinking maybe that little girl she's got locked away deep down inside hasn't gotten very far with her fairy tale because the whole damn world's been telling her to look for a prince, when really, all she wants is a cowboy."

Chapter 10

Friday and my mother couldn't get here soon enough. I'd finally pinned her down for a conversation several hours after I finished talking to Savannah.

"As always, I bow to the master. Having the wedding here at the lake house was genius."

"Then what's with the underlying tone of surprise?" My mother had her own version of the sweet girl giggle. Maybe it was a southern thing.

"Well, at first I thought you were just being lazy. Or maybe you just didn't have enough connections in Kentucky to get some hoity toity hall at such late notice. I mean, I know it'd be a one phone call fix back home, but they're probably not going out of their way to kiss your ass out here."

"Watch your language, Cal. I'm still your mother. And I'll have you know, people are always happy to kiss my ass no matter where I go. It's a nice ass, even at my age." I heard a quiet gulp. Wine time.

"I have to know. Is Jack there with you? Is he the one *uncorking* your bottle for you every night?" I was fully aware that he was gay, but I couldn't resist.

As expected, my mother gasped dramatically. "Calista, I'm not sure I appreciate what you're implying."

"Oh please, Ma. We all need to get *corked* from time to time." I laughed as I wandered over to my bed and fell back onto the mattress.

"Yes, I hear you've been getting your *corking* done on this trip," my mother said coyly.

"Don't get too excited. I sent Tyler packing the second he showed up," I laughed.

"I wasn't talking about Tyler, Cal. I was referring to Emerson."

I shot up straight from my bed. "Who have you been talking to?" Had to have been Noonie. Although, she didn't really know enough to imply that I was getting *corked* by anyone.

"Who do you think? Noonie. You really need to watch yourself around her. That nosy old goat has her eyes on everyone. And don't think for a moment when you're whispering about how cute you think he is, she can't hear you. That woman has better hearing than an owl hunting in the dark of night. And she'll squeal louder than a pig on slaughter day the second she has someone to tell."

"Um, you do realize you just made three animal references about your own mother, don't you? And, two of them were farm related. Slaughter day? What is happening to you?" I thought I even detected a slight twang in her voice toward the end there.

"Never mind that. I want to hear more about you and Emerson. I've been waiting for the sequel to that story for long enough. Now let's hear it."

"Why does everyone keep doing that? Acting like Emerson and I have some great romance written in the stars. Like we fell in love when we were kids or something. Emerson was sixteen. If he had fallen for a six year old that would have been a little sick, no?" I was well aware that *I* had been in love with him at six. And I could even understand why everyone would think that *I* would be falling for him again now. What I couldn't wrap my brain around was why everyone was so sure that he would feel the same. Obviously, I hoped this time around he would.

And he was certainly acting like it was a possibility. But, that was in no way magic related. It wasn't some epic soul mate tale of long lost lovers re-uniting. It was just a matter of a guy seeing a girl and thinking there might be something there. Right?

"You don't understand, Cal. You were too little, you wouldn't have seen it. And neither would Emerson. Even at sixteen he wouldn't have been able to recognize what everyone else could clearly observe between the two of you. It wasn't about falling in love. It was a connection. This strange, and inexplicable connection. And it wasn't just you being adorable and experiencing your first crush. Emerson was just as pulled in by you. And it wasn't sick or perverted in any way. It was sweet. Kind. Like you both recognized something in each other you didn't know in anyone else. I can't explain it, Cal. But we all knew something happened that summer. And I think many of us have been waiting and wondering if your paths would cross again as adults and what that connection would mean to you then."

My mother, the hopeless romantic. How could anyone argue with her when it came to love? She could sell a heart to the Grinch faster than a heart surgeon could sell one to a transplant patient.

"Ma. You can't do this. You can't drown me in all of your fairy tale crap. I'm already busy trying not to get sucked into my own." I sighed loudly. "Yes, there is something happening between Emerson and me. And yes, I am just as tempted to jump on the soul mate bandwagon, but the reality is, we hardly know each other and we live in completely different worlds. And…"

"And what?"

"And I'm scared enough as it is."

My mother was quiet for some time.

"How can you be scared? You're with Emerson. You'd follow him anywhere if he held out his hand for you to take."

I had nothing to counter with. Maybe because I was too afraid of what she'd come up with next if I tried to argue it any further.

Thankfully, my lack of response went down in her book as submission and we were able to move on to other topics. Such as Savannah's wedding. My mother confirmed that she would in fact be on a flight the next morning, so I was keeping my fingers crossed that this time, she would show. As often as Steph and I had given each other high fives and called each other the rock stars of wedding planning that afternoon after having successfully tasted cake and selected more wood structures to go with the arbor, we both knew we didn't really know shit about what we were doing.

Sure, for a brief moment it seemed like we had played a big part in bringing together the basics required to put on a good show, but all the other stuff, all the tedious little technicalities my mother could count off in her sleep, were completely beyond our scope of knowledge. Not to mention, my mother employed a staff of nearly twenty people. They were obviously coming to work every day to do *something*. And whatever that was, we certainly hadn't played any part in it.

No doubt my mother would bring her favorite little minion, Jack, along and he would have everything done in no time. He'd steal our rock star status right out from under us, but it was a sacrifice I was prepared to make. At least we'd still be able to take credit for the dress. Which still made us wedding day heroes in my book.

For the time being, all of my machine sewing was done and I was back to busying myself with the mind numbing task of attaching hundreds of little beads by hand. Beads were my nemesis. And while I hated them, I sort of loved them, too. There was no denying the elegance and beauty in the beaded details. Nor could I refute the fact that they served as a major creative outlet in terms of design possibilities. So, while I loved the beginning and the end of beadwork, it was the middle and most unavoidable aspect of attaching them, I sincerely detested.

I was about a third of the way done with the back piece when I heard a knock on the door.

"Come in," I mumbled through the needle I was holding in between my teeth.

It was Emerson.

"Were you planning on breaking for dinner?"

"Probably. Why? What time is it?" I searched the room for a clock but wasn't familiar enough with the space yet to know where to look.

Emerson grinned. "Almost eleven."

I spit out the needle. "Are you kidding me? I've been up here for over six hours?"

He nodded and stepped all the way into the room. He hadn't come empty handed either. In his left hand he was holding a small bottle of mineral water while the right was carrying a large plate covered in several slices of pizza.

"Steph ordered dinner in. Said you'd like it."

"Steph does know what I like." I had to smirk thinking about our previous conversation. "Thanks."

He handed me the plate and sat down in the small love seat across from me. I noticed he was freshly showered and even clean shaven, revealing a small scar on his chin I hadn't seen before.

"What happened there?" I asked, about to take a bite.

He reached up and rubbed the area with two fingers. "Met with the wrong end of a beer bottle."

"How exactly does something like that happen?" I asked, my curiosity piqued.

Emerson leaned back and settled into the cushions and I instantly felt happy knowing he would be staying for at least a little while.

"Well, this probably doesn't apply to everyone, but in my case, the bottle and I met during an argument with my ex-fiancée."

I almost choked on my pizza. Then I kinda wished I had so I wouldn't be able to hurl up what I had already eaten. "You were engaged?"

"I was. Does that matter?"

"No." *Yes!* "Anyway, you were saying about the bottle and your ex-" I couldn't get myself to say the word.

"I came home one night, found her wasted out of her goddamned mind, which wasn't unusual, and when I went to take the bottle from her, she fought me. The bottle got smashed and next thing I knew she was coming at me with it. Got me in the thigh pretty good, too." He automatically reached down to touch the spot just above his knee.

I was almost afraid to ask. "So what happened to her?"

"She tried to get help. Few times. Then, when she finally got clean, she left."

It sounded so simple. It also sounded really fucking complicated.

"Oh." I was twisting my fingers trying to decide how much more I wanted to know. "When did all of this happen?"

138

"We were together off and on all throughout our twenties, but it ended for good about four years ago." He sounded strangely callous as he spoke and I couldn't help but wonder if it was because he felt nothing or rather that he felt too much. But I wasn't about to ask him to clarify.

"I'm sorry."

Emerson stared blankly across the room. "Don't be. She sure as hell isn't."

It was the first time I'd ever seen that side of him. I'd thought I'd seen little signs of something, some sort of pain in his eyes even in spite of his usual carefree exterior, but I had just assumed it was something normal. And by normal I meant stupid stuff, like the way my parents' divorce had screwed me up. Surely his parents had fucked him up in one way or another. I mean, didn't they all? But no. This was no simple matter of mommy and daddy issues. This was some serious troubled shit. And most of it had taken place during the years of his life I had yet to experience in mine. Crap. It was like getting hit in the face with a frying pan TWICE. It was too much. My little Emerson fantasy was crumbling faster than a stale cookie, and it was leaving behind a nasty aftertaste.

"Hey." The quiet tone of his voice pulled me from the mental tornado ripping through my mind and leaving nothing but more questions in its wake. "I didn't mean to do that, just drop it all on you without warning. I mean, I knew you'd find out, this just isn't how I planned on telling you. But you asked…I didn't want you to think I was trying to hide anything from you."

My eyes focused again from their glazed state of waking coma and I could see him clearly. He wasn't relaxing on the sofa anymore. He was leaning forward on his knees, his hands folded, popping his knuckles nervously. He was worried.

Without thinking any further, I stood from my chair, crossed over to where he was, took his hands in mine and knelt down in front of him.

"In the interest of maintaining this full disclosure thing we've got going, all of what you just said basically scared the shit out of me. I'm just a fucking kid, compared to you. I freaked out when my boyfriend wanted a drawer at my place, I've certainly never entertained the idea of getting married. And the biggest issues we ever had were in regard to his inability to understand my need for punctuality and my inability to be a little less self-centered. I've never dealt with anything even comparable to addictions." I paused but kept my eyes locked onto his and suddenly my mother's words came rushing back. "Truth is, everything you just told me basically makes me want to run back to the city screaming. I'm a coward. I don't do brave things… Except when I'm with you." I hated it when she was right.

Emerson kissed my forehead, the tip of my nose and then found his way to my lips while slowly pulling me up toward him until I was sitting on his lap, my arms and legs wrapped tightly around him.

"The last thing I want to do is scare you," he whispered. "Feels like we're having some very serious conversations already for two people who probably ought to just be having fun."

"So this is just for fun?" I broke away to see his face.

"I said it ought to be." His lips were reaching up for mine. "But I haven't been able to stop thinking about you since I first saw you again in the back of that barn, with your hair blowing in the breeze and those dark brown eyes blazing at me. God, you took my breath away just standing there. Anyway, I'm here, still barely breathing, so it's probably more than just fun for me."

I held off his kiss a second longer. "Probably?"

His lips curved up playfully. "Definitely." Then there was no more escaping him. Nor did I want to as his lips crushed against mine and his arms wrapped around me tightly. I was back in that place, that little pocket of Emerson that seemed to be there just to hold me in it and I couldn't help but wonder what he did with the space when I wasn't there to fill it.

"I should probably let you get back to work before I get carried away here and find ways to distract you for the rest of the night," he murmured against my mouth, his hot breath brushing my skin, inviting me back for more in spite of what his words had just suggested.

"I could be okay with that." I flicked the tip of my tongue over his upper lip, reeling him back in to me. I could have spent hours kissing him. It was like our mouths were dancing together in perfect rhythm, moving to the same passionate song that seemed to build as it went on, heightening the emotions with each beat.

I found myself gripping him to me tighter, pressing him to my chest, my heart. Claiming him over all the others who had come before me. Because in my mind, he had been mine all along.

Suddenly, Emerson stood up from the sofa, still holding me molded to him. For a split second I thought we might be moving things over to the bed and my heart raced with anticipation. Only he stopped short and gently set me down in the chair I had occupied before climbing on top of him.

"What are you doing?" I asked, slightly out of breath from all of the previous excitement.

"Making sure I don't do anything that will make you pissed at me come morning." He leaned his forehead to mine, closed his eyes and sighed loudly. Damn him and his stupid self-control. "I'd really hate for you to dump me two days in because I made you late for something, and you would definitely be late getting that dress done if we keep doing what we're doing." He pulled back and slowly stood upright.

"Oh sure, tease me more why don't you?" I whined as his body continue to detangle from mine. "Fine, you're right."

"Yeah, I know." He grinned at me in that way only Emerson could and it was all I could do not to lunge for him all over again. I had no idea what was happening to me, but whatever it was, I liked it.

"What are you doing now?" I watched as he made his way back over to the sofa and stretched out on it.

"Relaxing." He propped up his feet on the end and crossed both arms behind his head.

"You're just going to lie there....while I'm working?"

"Yeah." He scooted himself further into the cushions until he was comfortable.

"Okay then." I picked up the dress and went back to my beadwork.

For a while we sat in silence as my focus on my stitching increased. I hadn't even noticed he was watching me.

"It's hard to believe you can create a design like that attaching one tiny little bead at a time. Have you always wanted to do this?"

I kept my eyes on my work. "Make wedding dresses? Yeah, I guess so. I mean, if there was a market for making lavish ball gowns, I probably would have gone with that, but since no one over the age of nine seems to want to dress like a Disney princess anymore, this was as close as I could get."

He chuckled. "Well, it seems to have worked out for you. Not that it happened by accident. Noonie's been talking about you designing dresses for at least as long as I've been working for her. She said you were, what? Eight? And already drawing up your first dress."

I lifted my head as the memory flashed through my mind bringing a smile to my lips. "Actually, I was six when I drew my first dress." Then without meeting his gaze, I turned back to my work.

"Oh yeah? Six and already thinking about weddings? Isn't that a bit young?" He pulled himself up onto his side to get a better view of me.

"No way. Girls start thinking about weddings way before six. Trust me, I had my first groom picked out when I was only three."

He actually sat up straight and brought his feet around to the floor again. "What? Three? Who were you going to marry when you were three?"

I grinned. "Prince Eric."

"What? Who is Prince Eric? Some European Royal?"

"Not exactly. He's from The Little Mermaid. Ariel's Prince Eric."

Emerson smirked. "I don't know what's working against you more. The fact that he's clearly already taken, or the fact that he's animated."

I tossed a scrap of material at him. "Shut it! I was three. I'm sure you had some less than realistic aspirations at the time."

"Sure did. I wanted to own Mr. Ed. Actually, I wanted to have a whole ranch with all talking horses. I was super bummed when that didn't pan out."

"See, now that's ridiculous…and totally adorable." I finished the back section and reached down for the hem of the dress, making sure I kept my hands busy since they were all too willing and wanting to go and reach for Emerson in an effort to aid my mouth in touching his again.

"That's me. Ridiculous and totally adorable." He settled back into his previous lounging position and I wondered if he was undergoing the same battles with temptation as I was.

"So, you always wanted to work with horses." I reached up and pulled down a pouch of beads I had pinned into my hair earlier.

Emerson shook his head. "No. The Mr. Ed thing was short-lived. I went through a whole slew of dream jobs before I was ever old enough to get one. Then, at twenty-four, I found myself suddenly in urgent need of a job and when Spence caught wind of it, he went straight to your Grandmother. She was always looking for people to do odd jobs around the place and she took me on right away. Kind of worked my way up from there. Guess you could say the horse thing sort of happened by accident."

I couldn't believe it. "But Noonie Skeeter says you're amazing with those horses. That sort of talent doesn't just happen by accident Emerson."

"No, it happens out of desperation and with lots and lots of practice." He was smiling, but I could tell by his tone that he was only half joking.

"Then if it hadn't been horses, what would you have done? Or, what would you want to do now?" I glanced at him and wondered if his answer would have him wearing those same jeans and tan muscles.

"No idea. But there's no changing it. This is it for me now. I can't imagine doing anything else with my life than what I'm doing. Nothing else fits."

I knew that feeling. My father had tried plenty of times to sway me from my goals of working in fashion. He'd wanted something more steady and secure. Responsible. Even now, he was constantly forwarding me emails from head hunters looking for people to fill corporate positions. I wasn't qualified for any of them, so I wasn't really sure what the point was. Either way, I'd gotten in the habit of simply deleting them as they came in.

"Well, I'm really glad Noonie hired you back then. I'm even happier you discovered your little horse whispering thing, accident or not…it worked out pretty well for me."

"It was a lucky accident." He winked at me.

"It really was." I reached down for more dress. At this rate I'd be done with the whole thing come morning. All because I needed the constant distraction for my hands and eyes to keep from attacking Emerson with my mouth and devouring him whole.

It was a good thing Steph hadn't been anywhere near that conversation. She probably would have hauled off and slapped me. But then, she hadn't just been right about

Liss getting scared. She'd been right about the other thing, too. The more important thing. The thing that was drawing her to me, and me to her. The thing neither of us had really ever had before. There was a word for what that was, but I wasn't about to use it yet.

Chapter 11

When I woke up the next morning, I was lying in Emerson's arms on the floor beside the love seat he'd been sitting on for most of the night while I worked on Savannah's dress. By the time I had finally stopped, it was after four o'clock in the morning.

Amazingly enough, Emerson had stayed up with me all throughout, talking to me, making me laugh and keeping my senses keen enough to keep stitching. Then, after the last bead had found its place, I had draped the gown back over the mannequin and happily fallen into this arms.

Since the loveseat hadn't been nearly big enough even for just him, we wound up sliding to the floor, giggling all the way down and not stopping until we fell asleep, my head to his chest, his heartbeat to my ear.

My eyes were barely open when I heard the sound of a loud engine pulling up out in the driveway. I searched for the clock and was once again, unsuccessful. How long had we been sleeping? Was it possible my mother and Savannah were already here?

I sat up, trying to get my bearings.

"Where do you think you're going?" Emerson grumbled, his eye lids still sealed shut.

"There's someone here." I stopped to listen again. The sound was gone, but I was sure I'd heard a car. Actually a truck was probably more like it.

"It's just Blake." His fingers laced up into my hair, twirling the strands hanging down against my back.

147

"Who?"

"My buddy, Blake. He's gonna help me finish up the woodwork for Savannah's wedding. Remember?"

Just barely. "Oh. Then shouldn't you be getting up to greet him or something?"

He shook his head, gently tugged at my hair to guide me back down toward him. Our lips were already touching when he said, "Let Steph welcome him. I'm sure he'd much rather see her anyway."

"I'm good with that." And then, at last, there was no more talking.

Nearly half an hour later we finally emerged from my bedroom and made our way down to the kitchen where we found Steph and Blake having a friendly chat over donuts and coffee.

Blake nodded at Emerson when he saw us. "I brought breakfast." He pointed at the carton of fresh Krispy Kremes.

"Blake, I like you already," I reached for my own ring of deep-fried sugar.

"And you must be Calista." He held out his non-coffee holding hand to me and I shook it while casually giving him the once over. Blake looked younger than Emerson. Not by much. He was probably still in his late twenties though. He had short blond hair and was built like a swimmer. Not that I knew any of those, but I'd watched the Olympics on TV and those dudes were all put together the same way. Super lean with massive arms and chests.

I turned toward Stephanie whose eyes had apparently traveled the same path mine had only from the other side. I grinned when she finally looked up and saw me staring at her. She went bright red almost instantly.

"Thanks for letting him in, Steph."

"Someone had to. Clearly it wasn't going to be either one of you." She handed Emerson and me two cups of coffee. A nice gesture, but I knew it was motivated only by wanting to keep her eyes busy and focused on things other than Blake's ass.

"Yes, well, we were up all night working on Savannah's dress," Emerson said, reaching for his second donut which he proceeded to dunk into his coffee.

I cocked my head to the side and peered up at him. "I'm sorry, we?"

"I was definitely up all night." He gave a little sideways nod. "*Watching* her work on Savannah's dress."

"Sure, that's what you two were doing," Stephanie mocked.

"No really. The dress is pretty much done. I mean, it's not done, done, but you know. It's done."

Blake peered back and forth between Steph and me and then turned to Emerson. "Did you understand that?"

"No. Hey, want to go play with some power tools?"

"Didn't bring my miter saw for nothing."

Steph and I watched as both boys walked from the kitchen talking about saws like they were five and comparing hot wheels collections. I was about to call her out on her obvious interest in Blake's rear end when Emerson came running back in.

"You forget something?"

"Sure as hell did." I didn't have to ask what. His arm was already around my waist, pulling me in for a long, sweet kiss. Then, as he let go, he smacked my ass and took off again. Leaving me behind with a dopey grin on my face.

"So, you're into spanking now," Steph said dryly as she started packing up what was left of breakfast.

"Never mind my ass. Let's talk about Blake's." I blocked her path back to the fridge. "What's up with the two of you?"

"Nothing." She put the box of donuts back on the counter. "We just met."

"Uh-huh. How long before you meet the rest of him?"

"Calista!"

"What? I know you want to see what else he has in those jeans aside from that tight little tush."

"First of all, hell yeah. And second of all, keep your eyes off of his ass."

I laughed. "They haven't been anywhere near there. Didn't have to be to know that he was built as nice from behind as he is from the front. The expression on your face while your eyes were locked on it, said it all."

"Anyway. Moving right along. If you're done with the dress, what are we going to do until your Mom and Savannah get here this afternoon?"

I held up my phone. "Got a text from my mom. She's got another assignment for us."

"Oh?" I could tell Steph was disappointed we'd be leaving. So was I.

"She made up some new and updated invites to send out to let people know about the change of venue since all the original ones said the wedding would be at the Gillespie, which you know, was never actually booked. Ah, gotta love a runaway wedding planner." I made face. "Anyway, she had a local shop print them up and she needs us to go pick them up. Well, technically it probably wouldn't take two of us to do it, but if I can't sit here and stare at Emerson be all manly with his power tools then you can't spend the day eyeballing Blake either. So, let's go.

Plus, we can go track down some linens for draping those window thingies they're making."

"Let's do this then. You know, so we can hurry up and get back." She wiggled her eyebrows playfully. Oh, I knew exactly what she was saying.

The entire week that followed compiled into one massive blur starting the moment my mother and Savannah arrived later that afternoon. From then on, everything had been wedding related and neither Steph nor I had been able to shirk any of the duties we were suddenly saddled with.

We didn't end up leaving after the weekend to head back to the farm, as originally planned. While Jack had accompanied my mother as suspected, there were still about a million little things that needed to be done, now that everyone was finally in the same place, and my mother wasn't about to let anyone break away.

So, when I wasn't fitting the dress and making the needed adjustments or taking all eleven bridesmaids dress shopping, which naturally led to dress altering, I was making table centerpieces, turning mason jars into lanterns and producing five hundred wedding favors for the guests consisting of tiny burlap sacks, each filled with two tulip bulbs and tied with a hand written thank you card and a set of three ribbons. To say I suffered from severe hand cramping by the time everything was all said and done would have been an understatement.

Still, in the midst of all the craziness, Emerson and I were stealing time to be together every night, even if it was only to fall asleep in each other's arms.

Then, at last, it was the night of the dress rehearsal and everyone cleared out to head back to Lexington where my aunt and uncle were hosting a massive dinner party. In spite of Savannah's insisting that Stephanie was like family already and was more than welcome to attend, she opted to take Blake up on his offer to show her around town for the night instead.

The rehearsal was being held in one of the trendiest restaurants in the city. The only reservation that had actually been made throughout this entire wedding fiasco because Savannah's mother had insisted on taking care of all of the arrangements herself.

Even though Emerson and I hadn't actually discussed going together, I naturally assumed that we would be, considering we had just spent the last ten days being more or less inseparable.

So, it was strange when I arrived with my mother and grandparents and found myself standing alone in a sea of people, most of whom I barely recognized. A problem no one else seemed to be having as they all mingled and chatted happily with one another, including my mother.

In fact, my mother appeared to be unusually social even by her standards when she ran into an old friend. Or, at least I suspected that's what he was. He didn't have any of the trademark Ashcraft traits, nor was he wearing a wedding band, so even though he could easily have been an uncle I simply didn't know, it wasn't likely. And I was going with that, because he was hot.

Well, for an older guy. Like a Kevin Costner hot. Not like 'I would actually want to do him' hot, but like 'I clearly had some daddy issues' hot. Anyway, my mother seemed to think so, too. That he was hot, not that I had daddy issues. And in her case, it was probably more of the 'actually doing him' hot sort of way.

I was so fascinated watching my mother interact with a man who wasn't thirty years younger than her or a homosexual that I didn't even notice when Emerson finally showed up.

"Wow," he whispered in my ear as he placed his hand on my waist to guide me closer to him.

"I was starting to think you weren't coming."

"Sorry. Just got caught up in some groomsmen business."

"I didn't know you were a groomsman." But then we had made a point not to discuss the wedding at all considering it had already consumed the bulk of our existence in the past two weeks.

"Yeah, Spence, Simon and I are all part of the wedding party." He didn't look particularly excited about it.

"So, who are you walking down the aisle?" I scanned the room curiously. I had already met all the bridesmaids since I'd been in charge of dressing them all.

Emerson turned his head, "Shauna."

Shauna. Shauna. Oh, right. "The blonde with the tattoo on her shoulder. Savannah had a fit about it. Apparently tattoos weren't a part of the look she was going for." I grinned. Brides got hung up on the weirdest things.

"Yeah, that's her." He shifted back and forth uncomfortably and his hold on me seemed to loosen. "Hey, remember I told you I was engaged a while back?"

No. "That's her?" The words barely came out.

"Yeah." He looked painfully uncomfortable. Only I couldn't tell if it was on her behalf, mine or his own.

"How?"

"She's married to the groom's little brother now. Small world, huh?"

"No shit." The wheels in my head were turning rapidly as I tried to collect all of the information I had come in contact with regarding this woman since arriving in Kentucky. Then it hit me. Shauna was a mom. She had a daughter. My mind was racing. How old had Savannah said she was? It had to be less than four, right? No. There had been talk of school. Talk of a dance. Next year? Yes. Shauna had joked about saving her bridesmaid's gown for her. First dance. When was that? Sixth grade? So, she was eleven? No, younger. Ten. Maybe nine.

Panic struck me as I counted back the years during which Emerson had said they'd been together. Then, as if he'd been reading my mind, his two fingers came up under my chin, gently raising my gaze to meet his eyes.

"Mackenzie isn't my daughter. Shauna was pregnant already when we got together."

I waited, but there was no moment of relief. "Oh." Then, something inside me shifted. I stepped back, out of Emerson's arms. Suddenly, they didn't feel so safe anymore.

"Liss." He tried to take my hand again, but I moved it before he could reach it.

"No," I whispered, shaking my head as I turned and started to walk from the room, gaining speed the further I got from him.

Before I knew it I was out in the parking lot with nowhere to go. Face to face with nothing but cars as far as the eye could see and the black of night, a sob escaped me. I buried my face in my hands, closing my eyes and trying to shut out the world, or at the very least, Kentucky.

When I finally got ahold of myself again, I took a deep breath and prepared to head back to the restaurant in hopes that someone inside would be able to find me a cab. With all the determination I could muster, I spun myself back around. And there he was. Emerson.

"What are you doing out here?" My voice sounded strange. Hollow.

"You're out here." As if it was that simple.

"I think you missed the point of my dramatic exit." I directed my gaze back at the cars. They were easier to look at.

"No, I got it. You were making a run for it. That was pretty clear."

"Yeah, well, you've kind of ruined the gesture by following me." The emptiness was quickly filling up with anger.

"What about what you're ruining by running out? Huh?"

Automatically my head turned toward him, challenged by his words, and then instantly defeated by the look in his eyes. He was in pain. *I* was causing him pain. But then he had hurt me, too.

"You should have told me. You let me walk in here and be completely blindsided. You had to have known she would be here. Had to have known I'd find out, that I'd put it all together. You should have done it for me." I wanted to shout. Wanted to scream and unleash the fury building up within me, but I didn't.

"I know. I know I should have told you. I wanted to. But when I first told you about Shauna…I saw the panic in your eyes. And you admitted it. You told me yourself that you were ready to bolt." He looked almost helpless.

"Yes, but I didn't. I stayed. Because of you. Because I believed that I was safe with you. No matter what."

"You are."

"No. I'm not. Not when I can walk into a room and find myself face to face with your ex-fiancée and find myself adding and subtracting the years trying to determine if you're a father or not."

He sighed. "I told you, she's not my daughter."

"Yeah. Technically. But you were with her mother while she was pregnant. You were going to marry her. On some level, you must have felt like she was." My eyes were locked onto him now, searching for some sign, anything that would explain to me what had happened. Why he had chosen to keep something so big from me, especially when my finding out had been inevitable. But he had lowered his own gaze and was staring at the ground.

"Lissy." When he finally looked up again, his eyes were glazed with the threat of tears. "We've had less than two weeks together and two decades of life to catch up on. There are a million things about me I haven't told you yet, but that doesn't mean I don't intend to. Yes, I knew you'd find out about Shauna tonight. And yeah, I knew it was possible that you knew she had a child and that you would wonder what part I had played in that. But Shauna and Mackenzie are not a part of my life I enjoy talking about. And I wasn't prepared to taint the happiness I've felt with you until it was absolutely necessary. Clearly, I misjudged the timing." He took several steps toward me and this time, I didn't try to back away. "Shauna was three months pregnant when I met her. I was twenty-four, working in construction. She was alone and living in her car in a lot near the jobsite I was on. She'd left her boyfriend when she found out she was pregnant. He'd been abusive in the past and she was afraid of what he might do to the baby." He was biting the inside of his cheek. "Thing is, my mother went through the same thing. Before she started working as Spence's nanny, we'd gone back and forth between shelters and an old Chevy impala for two years."

156

I held my breath listening to him speak. It didn't matter what else he had to say. I'd already forgiven him.

"When Shauna first moved in, we weren't a couple. We barely knew each other. I was just helping her out and then things just evolved. Honestly, Liss, I don't know that I ever really loved her, but she needed me. There was the baby, and then postpartum depression...only we were both so young and we didn't know...things got bad and she spiraled out of control and started drinking. By the time I understood what had happened, she had a problem with booze. It was a mess, Liss. And then there was Mackenzie. And wouldn't you know it, she had these big brown eyes..." A bittersweet smile formed on his lips. "And I couldn't help but be reminded of the little girl with pigtails from that summer at the lake house who had first taught me what it meant to be needed. And, so, I stayed with Shauna. I became the kind of man they could both depend on. But none of that mattered, because really, neither one of us was in love with the other. We'd just been going through the motions for so long we'd lost sight of it somewhere along the way."

For a moment I was certain she'd walk away. Maybe she should have. Maybe I deserved it. I hadn't lied to her, but I hadn't exactly been honest either. Not because I was trying to deceive her, but because I was afraid she would look at me differently. Look at me the way she was doing now.

"What happened to Mackenzie? Do you still talk to her?"

It wasn't the kind of question I had expected, although, all things considered, I should have.

"Not anymore. I did. I didn't want to just disappear out of her life, I mean, I'd been there from the day she was born...but when things got serious between Shauna and Ryan, I knew it was causing problems for them. Causing problems for Mack. I'm not her dad. I'm never going to be. But Ryan is now. He adopted her, made it official after the wedding." It hadn't been easy. I may not have loved Shauna the way I should have, but I had always loved Mackenzie as if she was my own. Especially in the years when Shauna had been too messed up to take care of her and it had all fallen on me. Mack and I had been through hell and back together, only she would never remember it. In the end, letting go was the best thing I could do for her.

"I'm sorry."

I was confused. My mind had been wandering. Maybe she had said something else and I had missed it. What on earth would she be apologizing for?

"What?"

"I'm sorry." She said it again.

"Liss?"

Her face softened. No smile, but her eyes gazed at me with the same warmth I'd grown so accustomed to from her. "I get it. I understand why you didn't tell me. And I'm not mad, but I don't know if I can do this."

I took a small step toward her and it took an insane amount of restraint to stop there.

There were tears in her eyes as she turned and walked away a second time. Watching the distance between us grow with each step she took filled my chest with a sensation that made me feel like I'd been kicked by one of the horses. It was painful and it took my breath away and I knew it was only the beginning. This was what losing her would feel like. Only, I hadn't lost her. Not yet. She just needed time. Or, at least that's what I told myself.

Chapter 12

The remainder of the evening passed me by in a haze. I didn't see Emerson again the rest of the night, but that didn't really make matters any easier.

By the time we got back to Ashcraft Farms I was exhausted and ready to bury my face in my pillow for a good cry. But first, I needed to make a pit stop in the kitchen for something sweet and fattening. Pattie was bound to have a stash of baked goods somewhere. It didn't take me long to find it either. The air was still filled with the sweet scent of brownies when I walked in.

I was busy piling up brownie chunks in a large bowl and smothering them in chocolate syrup and ice cream when Noonie Skeeter walked in and I stared back at her like a deer caught in the headlights.

"Rough night, darlin'?" She smiled warmly and squeezed my chocolate dispensing hand, gently lowering it back down to the counter.

"I was just in the mood for something sweet." And enough chocolate to send a bear into a diabetic coma.

"Alright, if that's all it is, I won't say another word about it. But, before I let you go for the night, I will tell you this. We don't choose our soul mates. We don't choose who they are or when they show up in our lives. We don't choose the circumstances or the settin'. It just happens. The only choice we have is whether we acknowledge it or not and if it's worth the fight. The most spectacular things in life are rarely easy, Calista. Simple perhaps, but never easy." She paused. "Ask your mama sometime. She'll tell you."

I had no idea how to respond after any of that. As much as I had toyed around with the idea of Emerson and I being destined in some way, it sounded more than just a little dramatic coming from my grandmother. And what was she implying about my mother? The only soul mate she'd ever eluded to had been herself. It certainly hadn't been my father and she had made zero effort after the divorce to find anyone else.

Apparently, Noonie wasn't waiting for an answer from me. She just poured herself a glass of water, kissed my cheek and then left again without saying another word.

Feeling even more confused than I already was, I meandered out of the kitchen and made my way up the stairs. Walking down the hallway toward my bedroom, I passed the room my mother was supposed to be staying in. The door was ajar and the lights were out.

I knocked and slowly slid it open all the way. "Ma? You in here?"

The room was completely empty and the light in the attached bath was also out. There was no sign of her anywhere. Which could only lead me to one conclusion. She was waiting for me in *my* room likely planning to dole out her own version of wisdom same as Noonie had down in the kitchen.

I put a giant spoonful of brownie into my mouth and made my walk of surrender down the hall in preparation of what lie ahead. Only my room was just as dark and deserted as hers had been. She had to be here somewhere and unless she was bunking with Noonie and Poppy for the night, there was really only one other place left to look.

I felt like Belle in Beauty and the Beast as I made my way up to the third floor as if I was entering the forbidden west wing of the castle. Sure enough, when I arrived upstairs, there was a sliver of light shining out from below the door of my mother's childhood room.

Rapping my knuckles across the wood as I turned the knob, I let myself in.

"Ma?"

She was sitting on her old bed, not really doing anything. Just sitting.

"I hope you brought a second spoon," she said eyeing my bowl.

"No, but I can go get one." I was halfway out the door again.

"It's fine. You look like you need it more than I do anyway." She patted the mattress beside her for me to come and sit.

"What are you doing up here? Little trip down memory lane?" Even with her sitting smack dab in the middle of it all, I still couldn't imagine my mother actually living in this room.

"Something like that." She smiled, but there was a strange sadness in her eyes and I couldn't help but wonder if it was tied to the unsettling vibe I got every time I walked through that doorway.

"Ma, what died in here?" I was half joking as I pointed at the dreary drapery which clearly added to the haunted ambiance of the space.

Her response was the last thing I expected.

"I did." She sighed heavily. "Or at least, a part of me."

"What are you talking about?" Was I about to find out exactly why my mother had abandoned Kentucky and every Ashcraft with it?

She glanced down at my bowl and using her two fingers scooped out a glob of chocolate and ice cream which she then dropped into her mouth in what was the least sophisticated gesture I'd ever witnessed from her.

"That was ladylike," I mumbled.

She grinned. "I've got no one left to impress." She sucked her thumb loudly, removing any leftover chocolate. "I guess now is as good a time as any to tell you. Honestly, I'm surprised you didn't stumble upon this little bit of history on your own already. On second thought, it's probably still swept under the rug in true Ashcraft fashion." She stood up from the bed and walked over to an old bookcase in the corner of her room. For a moment she just stood there. Then, slowly she reached up and retrieved a picture frame from the top shelf. Those things seemed to be hidden everywhere around here.

"When I was eighteen I met a boy named Jake. His father was Dan Rimmel, our feed supplier back then. After high school, Jake started working for him making deliveries, and so he and I crossed paths."

"I take it Jake was your first love?" I had a spoon full of brownie and ice-cream in my hand but wasn't entirely sure whether or not it was appropriate to eat under the circumstances.

"Jake was more than my first love. He was my only love." She glanced down at the picture in her hands longingly. Without even turning in my direction she said, "Cal you'll be wearing that soon if you don't stick it in your mouth already."

How did she always do that?

"Ma," my mouth was full now, having followed orders automatically, "if you were so in love with him, what happened?"

"Our families. Poppy had a shit fit when he found out. Said no daughter of his was going to marry the feed guy. Meanwhile, Jake's mom was beside herself when she heard about us because I wasn't exactly the sweet little girl she had envisioned for her baby boy."

I peered over at her skeptically. My mother was the most sophisticated and proper woman I had ever met. "Who did she want him to marry? Little Debbie?"

She laughed. "Not exactly, but close. I know me being your mom and all it's probably hard for you to imagine me being any other way than I've been since you've known me, but the truth is, I was quite the wild child in my younger years."

I twisted my mouth to keep from laughing. Of course she noticed.

"It's true, Cal. Make fun of me all you want, but I was trouble. Not just because I was runnin' around with a boy my father didn't like, but in general. I was loud and strong-willed. Took a lot of risks. Ask Noonie Skeeter. I made her crazy for a long time."

"So then what happened?"

"Jake broke up with me." She came and sat down next to me again. "We were all set to take off together. Start our own lives. Away from everyone telling us what we could and couldn't do. Then, the night we were supposed to leave I stood out by the gate, my bags packed, waiting for him to come and get me, only when he finally showed up it was to say good bye."

She was keeping it together in true Sophie Luvalle fashion, but I could tell that her heart was aching even after all these years.

"Why?"

She shrugged, lips pressed together tightly. "Said that our parents were right. Not for the reasons they thought, but for reasons he couldn't ignore any longer.

165

When I tried to argue with him, he just went silent. Stone cold. It hurt worse than anything he could have said to me. So, I said good bye and watched him drive off into the night without me."

I was holding my breath. "Then what?"

"Then I marched my pissed off ass back up to the house, stole the keys to Poppy's truck and never looked back."

I couldn't believe it. After all this time, I finally understood. "You left for New York that night?"

She nodded. "Poppy was mad as hell, but Noonie Skeeter kept him from coming after me. I think she'd known all along I was leaving with or without Jake. Only difference was, now I wasn't too keen on ever coming back."

She handed me the picture she'd been holding this entire time. It was my mother. She was laughing and wrapped up in the arms of a man. It was strange to see her with someone other than my father. Even stranger when I realized I'd never seen her that happy during all the years they'd been married.

"Do you ever regret it?"

"No." She took my hand and looked me straight in the eyes. "I could never regret anything that led me to you, Calista."

It was so like her to make me feel better in the midst of her own heartbreak. My gaze dropped back down to the picture. "Hey. Wait a minute. I know this guy. He was at the party tonight! You were talking to him! Oh my GOD! Was that the first time you'd seen him since the night he dumped you?"

She made a face. "Gee, thanks for being so tactful with your choice of words, Cal. Yes, that was Jake tonight.

And yes, it was the first time I'd seen him in twenty-five years."

My eyes were still wide from the realization. "What did he say? What was it like?"

"He said a lot of things, none of which I'm going to repeat to you. And, it was strange at first, but then he laughed and it was still him. The same boy I fell in love with once upon a time."

She smiled, but it was bittersweet.

"Ma?"

"Yes?"

"I think I'm in love with Emerson." It was the first time I'd said the words out loud. Hearing them was even scarier than saying them. But, apparently only for me.

"Yes, I think you are." She took the picture from me and returned it to the top shelf of her bookcase. Then she came to stand in front of me. "The question is, what are you going to do about it?"

"I don't know," I whined as I threw myself back onto her bed dramatically. "He has all this baggage. All this...stuff! Ex-fiancées, and almost daughters! He's older than I am and he's had all of this extra life. Life without me in it."

My mother came and laid beside me, only she was far more graceful about it. "Cal, you can hardly hold his age against him. It's not his fault he was born too soon. And this whole mess with him and Shauna, well, I think it says a lot about the kind of man he is."

"Wait. You knew about him and Shauna?"

"Well, yeah. What, you think I haven't been keeping tabs on him all this time?"

I shot straight up again. "What? What does that even mean?"

She reached up and pressed my shoulder down until I was even with her again. "Relax. It's not like he knew about it. But, hell yeah I was keeping tabs on him. What, you think I didn't know this day would come? I knew sooner or later, life would bring you back out here, bring you two together, and I wanted to know what you would find when it did."

"Well way to be on top of things! He damn near married somebody else!"

She waved it off dismissively. "He was never going to marry her."

"How can you say that? They were engaged!"

"But for all the wrong reasons. Trust me. If I know one thing, it's couples. More importantly, couples who will and won't make it down the aisle. And Shauna and Emerson were never even close."

I cocked my left brow at her. "What, you're like the wedding psychic now?"

"I don't know why you're saying it like it's a new thing." She was looking at me like she was suppressing a grin. "Go ahead. Ask me."

"Ask you what?"

"If you and Emerson will make it down the aisle. You know you want to."

"I absolutely do not." I rocked myself up and to my feet. I was nearly out the door when I stopped and turned back. "Thank you for telling me all of that. And, I'm really sorry you had your heart broken."

"Don't be. My heart mended the day I got you."

I smiled at her. Suddenly, I felt like I understood her in a whole new way.

The drive home from the party felt like the longest ride of my life. The sudden silence gave me too much time to rehash the night's events and the conversations that should have happened way before tonight.

It wasn't easy, but I forced myself to pass the farm and keep on driving even though all I wanted was to go and find Liss. To hold her in my arms and tell her anything and everything she wanted to know and needed to hear to feel safe again with me. Instead, I pulled into my driveway and headed up toward the house. I hadn't left a single light on. Since I'd planned on making it a late night, I'd left Reesie back at the farm with the other dogs. Only now, her company would have made a world of difference.

I was barely through the front door when my phone rang.

"Yeah?"

"Emerson? Her Tethered Wings is foaling. Think it might be breached. What do you want us to do?"

It was Marcus, a newbie. Burke was likely just headed home from the party himself. Shit.

"Call the vet. I'll be over as fast as I can."

In no time flat I was back in my truck and driving up to the house I'd swore I wouldn't come back to tonight. Thankfully, I had all the reason I needed to veer left for the barn before I ever made it close enough for Liss to hear my truck.

Two hours later and we'd been able to deliver the foal safely. The vet had rolled up just after and was able to check out both horses and assure us that both had made it through the tumultuous delivery without any permanent damage.

Burke had arrived about halfway through, although he hadn't been much help. Too much booze at the party had rendered him pretty useless. Even now, as the buzz was wearing off, his eyes had that glazed look as he chatted up the vet, thanking him for coming out and saying good bye. He'd be back in the morning anyway to check on one of the colts in training. He'd come up lame the day before.

"Enjoyed the party tonight, didn't you old man?" I joked as he joined me in the office where I was busy filling out the birth report.

"Sure did. Who knew it would end in a crisis? I take off maybe one night every ten years and this is what happens. Just another reason retirement can't come soon enough." He tapped his hip thoughtfully. "You still sure you want the gig, kid?"

"Hell yeah. Shit, Burke, how much did you have to drink tonight?" I shook my head laughing at him.

"Oh, it's not that. I just thought maybe you were havin' second thoughts. You know, now that you've been spendin' all this time with Troy's granddaughter."

I put the file down and leaned back in the chair. This ought to be interesting. "What does Calista have to do with any of this?"

"So it's true then? You two are an item?"

"Honestly, right now I don't even know." I ran my hands over my face trying to wipe away any trace of my struggles over the situation with Liss and me.

Burke shrugged. "Maybe that's your out then."

"What? What out? I don't want an out, Burke. I'm in love with this girl."

His face fell. "Are you sure she's worth it? I mean, I know she's pretty and doin' big things with her life back in the city. But are you ready to be a kept man? Live the rest of your life in her shadow?"

Nothing Burke was saying was making any sense. "What the hell are you talking about Burke?"

He tilted his head down, like he was dreading being the bearer of bad news. When he finally looked me in the eye, his expression was grim. "You have to know that old Troy would never go for this. Sure, he thinks the world of you...when it comes to his horses. But don't think for a second that same high regard will transfer on to his granddaughter. Certainly didn't with his own daughter."

He couldn't be serious. Troy Ashcraft was stubborn and old school in many ways, but this?

"You're saying I need to choose. Calista...or this job?" The choice was easy. Jobs were a dime a dozen. There was only one of Liss.

"I'm sayin', losin' your job will be the least of your worries if you pursue this thing with Calista any further," he paused. "You never heard about what happened back in the day with Jake Rimmel did you?"

I shook my head. What did our feed supplier have to do with any of this?

"Jake started workin' for his dad when he was eighteen. He drove a truck for him, makin' deliveries. Well, wasn't too long before he caught Sophie's eye. She was young, beautiful and the wildest spirit Ashcraft Farms has ever seen. Once she set her sights on Jake, that poor boy didn't have a chance."

"Sophie. Sophie Luvalle. She's the wild child in love with the feed guy?"

"You'd never know it to look at her now, would ya? True though, every word. Story didn't end there either. Both their families had their own reasons for wantin' those two apart. It was a regular Romeo and Juliet tragedy, it was. Well, finally they both decided they'd had enough of fightin' with everyone and they hatched a plan to take off. Sneak out in the middle of the night when no one was around to stop them. Only someone did."

"Troy?"

"Troy. Old man never did miss a thing. He figured out what Sophie was plannin' and he went straight to Jake. Told him to end things with his daughter immediately. Said she had bigger and better things to do with her life than marry the feed guy. Said if he didn't do as he was told, Troy'd put Rimmel Feed out of business. He could've done it, too. Few calls, Rimmel would have lost his biggest accounts. Well, naturally, Jake couldn't let that happen."

I stared blankly across the room as my mind played back the last two weeks for me. "He let Sophie go."

"Sure did. And look at how her life turned out. Think she would have accomplished half as much if she'd have run off with Jake that night? Or, hell, even if they hadn't run off, if they'd stayed here, with the support of their families?" Burke shook his head. "No way."

I felt like the wind had been knocked out of me. It wasn't the same. Jake and Sophie were nothing like Liss and I. We weren't kids. We'd each been on our own career track for years. We were well on our way to finding success. How could Troy possibly have the same objections? Except of course, that no matter which way you spun it, I was the help. She was the heiress. It did sort of put things into an uncomfortable perspective.

"Just think about what I told you, kid. No need to make any decisions tonight. Hell, maybe not making any decisions at all will be best. Weddin's tomorrow. Let her go home. Back to the city. Won't be long before the distance sets in and day to day life takes over. With any luck, your time together will fade into nothin' more than a pleasant memory."

Burke gave me a nod good night and walked out. Not that there was much night left to be had. There certainly wasn't anything good about it.

Chapter 13

By the time I finally made it to sleep that night it was already time to get up again. Or, at least it felt that way when the alarm went off. I swear I'd only just closed my eyes a second earlier. Regardless, there was a wedding to put on and we had to make a four hour drive before we could even get started putting the finishing touches on everything before the guests arrived.

Thankfully, Jack, my mother's minion, had stayed behind at the lake house to keep the preparations in full swing until we got back.

After everything I'd learned the night before, there was now a list of people I didn't want to get stuck in a car with for four hours, so much so I was prepared to highjack Noonie's truck and make the drive myself again. Thankfully, it didn't come to that.

Steph and her P.A. psychic senses had swung by the farm even though Blake had already agreed to give her a ride. I wasted no time in jumping in the passenger seat and squeezing Steph into the middle. Not that I heard her complaining.

We'd been driving along for nearly an hour in complete silence when she apparently decided she'd had enough.

"Anything you want to talk about Cal?"

I shook my head, pushing out my lower lip and doing my best clueless look. "No."

"Really? Then why did you come running down the stairs, nearly tackling me in the process, to get out to the truck and jump in before I could even say good morning?"

"Um, because I foolishly believed that you had brought me coffee, that's why. Have you ever seen me run like that for anything else?" While I was on that, where the hell *was* the coffee?

"Cal." It was all she said. Like she was my freaking mother or something.

I twisted my mouth back and forth like a five year old who'd been ordered to admit she punched a boy for having cooties. Finally I threw my hands up in the air dramatically and let it all out.

"Holy shit, Steph! You have no idea. I mean, just seriously, NO IDEA! Let's start with little stuff, shall we? Like how my mother nearly eloped with the feed guy when she was eighteen. Oh yeah. Totally normal behavior for her back then. Uh-huh. And then of course, even though it didn't work out, she still considers him her one true love – which you know, says a lot about her marriage to my dad, but never mind that – and who could blame her. Even for an old guy, he's pretty damn hot. And I know that. Because I saw him. Yeah, Jake the feed guy was there. At the party. Last night." I had to take a brief break from my rant to take a few breaths. I was worried Steph would interrupt me and I would lose my steam, but apparently she was too stunned to say much of anything.

So, I continued, "That was just my mother's drama. I had plenty of my own. Did you know Emerson was engaged before? I know *you* did," I pointed my finger accusingly at Blake, "but did you? No? Yeah, well I did. What I didn't know was that his ex is one of Savannah's bridesmaids. Know what else I didn't know? That she has a daughter. Yeah. Was pregnant when they got together. Emerson practically raised her until they split four years ago. Let's see, am I forgetting anything? No, no I think that about covers it. Now then, can we all agree I deserve a goddamn cup of coffee?!"

"Starbucks. Now." Steph was waving her hand and belting out orders, but she never took her eyes off of me. "That…is fucking insane. Seriously. Like, I've got nothing else. Just. Wow."

Meanwhile, Blake stayed uncomfortably silent as he took the next exit in search of coffee.

"What? You think I'm being dramatic or something? Blowing things out of proportion?" I'd had all night to go over everything a million different times with zero outlet for all of the emotions running rampant within me. Blake wasn't the ideal target for them, but if he was going to side against me, even slightly, he would do the trick.

"Look, I don't want to get in the middle of whatever is going on between you and Emerson, but -"

"But what?" Now even Steph looked like she was about to pounce on him, and not in a good way.

"Well, you said you knew. I mean, he clearly wasn't keeping things from you. Maybe he didn't give you all the details, but if you had a story like that, would you go out of your way to share it?"

I had to close my eyes and take a deep breath. "I'm sorry, what now? How would telling me that his ex-fiancée was one of the bridesmaids have been going out of his way? Hm? I wasn't asking for a breakdown of their relationship. I didn't ask for a play by play of their first date, the proposal or the break up. All I wanted was a simple heads up. How is that asking too much?"

Blake was staring out of the driver's side window, probably wishing he could be on the other side of it. "You don't understand. A guy like Emerson has a lot of pride. He came from nothing. Not just nothing. He came from shit. His father was a top of the line asshole. Whether that was Emerson's fault or not, that kind of thing follows you around like a shadow you can't shake. A constant reminder of who you were predestined to be and desperately want to avoid becoming. He had to work twice as hard to become the kind of man the men he respected would accept and respect in return. And he did that. People look up to him now. They depend on him. Expect him to have the answers."

He stopped temporarily as he pulled into a parking spot outside of Starbucks and shifted into park. Then, he turned to face me. "In a million years a guy like Emerson would never expect to get a woman like you. And if by some miracle he had the chance, he would go out of his way to be the kind of man he felt was worthy of her. And if he had things in his past that could taint that image, jeopardize his one shot, why would he go out of his way to bring them to the forefront? He wouldn't. And not for the reasons you think. It wasn't about keeping secrets from you, Cal."

"Then what was it about? Explain it to me." I really, really wanted to understand.

He sighed heavily like he was about to tell me something he wasn't supposed to. Probably breaking all kinds of Bro Codes by doing so.

"Women are talkers, yes? We can all agree on that? Well, men, are not. And almost all of the most important things you express to us have nothing to do with the things you say. Hold on, I'm not done," he held up his hand to halt my impending argument. "My point is, men like the way their women look at them. We like to be praised, sure, but what we really like, what we bask in, is the way your eyes seem to stream an endless flow of love and pride, like we're fucking Superman and can always save the day. Because, ultimately, we all want to be your heroes. Now, I'm no relationship expert, but I'm just guessing you've been giving Emerson that 'you're my knight in shining armor' gaze since you got here. And, I think we can all agree, that logically, that light in your eyes might have dimmed some had he told you all there was to tell. It certainly seems to have been snuffed out altogether right now."

I turned my head toward Steph to see her reaction to Blake's big revelation, except her eyes were locked on him already, giving him a mad dose of 'you're my hero vision' right then and there. As a result he had about the dopiest grin on his face I'd ever seen. *Damn.*

"Blake studied psychology. He's a high school guidance counselor," she muttered dreamily.

"Well that explains why he dresses like a redneck, drives a shit truck and plays with power tools. Or not." My sarcastic mumblings were lost on both of them as they continued to give each other the googly eyes while I went inside for a massive jug of coffee.

The rest of the ride pretty much made me want to gag, or at least gesture gagging the entire time. It was clear that Steph was a goner. I had lost my top rating and been demoted thanks to Blake, the counselor in cowboy wear. I had mixed feelings about that and they were far less strenuous to deliberate than those concerning Emerson, so I happily gave them my undivided attention.

Once at the lake house it was easy to keep distracted. Jack was spewing orders at us left and right, and much to everyone's shock, including my own, I actually followed them. He could have his moment of glory. Besides, no one back home would ever believe him anyway.

My mother showed up shortly after us, along with the bride and all of her bridesmaids in tow. This was where things got slightly sticky. After all, I had to dress them all. Well, not literally, but I had to oversee the whole shebang and make sure no one suffered from any last minute wardrobe malfunctions. Thankfully, Steph was right there with me, every step of the way. More importantly, she acted as my shield, intercepting Shauna anytime she made her way in my direction.

The wedding itself went off without a hitch. Steph, Jack and I all stood in the back, watching like we were backstage hands at a major theater production, which weddings kind of were. Standing back there, I saw Emerson for the first time since I'd walked away from him the night before. He looked handsome in his black tux. Like, ridiculously handsome.

If he had been looking for me, it didn't show. He just seemed to stare blankly ahead, a sad sort of expression hiding behind his vacant smile. My heart ached just seeing him like that.

Then, at last it was over and the reception began. I made a beeline for the groomsmen hoping to find Emerson, only he wasn't with them. After wandering through the crowd of guests all mingling and catching up, I finally spotted him heading into the house. I couldn't have asked for a better opportunity.

I ran in through the French doors lining the wall to the pool and then stopped to listen. There was plenty of noise coming from the kitchen. The caterers were in high gear already. Maybe he had headed to his and Spence's old room.

I hurried down the hall and down the stairs that led to the basement. The door was open when I arrived at the end. There he was.

"Hey."

He smiled helplessly. "Hey yourself."

He looked lost. Not at all the confident strong man I knew him to be.

With every doubt being instantly obliterated, I flew across the room and into his arms. His mouth came down to greet mine, capturing my lips with such a tender force I knew I was his and he was mine. No amount of time, not past or future, could ever change that.

"I'm sorry," I breathed against his soft kiss.

"Liss, considering the situation and the role I played in it, I'm going to have to call dibs on all of the apologies." The smile was slowly coming back to his eyes and I felt my heart ache a little less.

"You're a jackass. And yes, you have plenty to apologize for. But so do I."

"Come again?"

"I never should have run out of there like that. It's just, I've never had anything in my life I wasn't prepared to walk away from. So, when things get uncomfortable, or don't go my way, I just...let it go."

"Are you saying...that you have something *now* that you're not prepared to walk away from?" His eyes were locked onto mine, daring me to answer truthfully.

"I'm saying, I now have *someone* that I'm not prepared to walk away from." It had been harder to admit than I'd anticipated, but once the words had been spoken I'd never felt happier.

He pulled me up into his arms, tight against him and still it wasn't close enough. Not near close enough.

181

"You want to get out of here?" he murmured into my ear.

"Yes." Anymore and my words would have led to propositioning him right then and there with the wedding party right outside the door.

My hand nestled safely in his again, we went to make our getaway. Only, we didn't get very far.

My mother and Jake were blocking our path.

Emerson and I were still out sight when we heard them having a heated argument out in the formal dining room. We stopped short in the hall, not wanting to interrupt. Not that eavesdropping wasn't just as rude. If not more so.

"Can you honestly tell me that you're happy, Jake? Running your father's business? You never wanted that! You were going to go to school. Become an architect. What happened to those dreams?" My mother's voice was filled with anguish.

"Those dreams weren't practical, Sophie. No one but you ever expected me to follow through with them." It was the first time I'd ever heard Jake's voice. It was raspy, but his tone was surprisingly tender in spite of the heightened emotions.

An unexpected sob escaped my mother. "Why, Jake? Why couldn't you just let me love you? All you needed was someone to love you enough to want better for you. To want for you what you wanted for yourself. Why couldn't you just let me give you that? Don't you know how easy that would have been for me?"

There was a sound of movement and I wondered if it was bringing them closer together or farther apart. Then, when Jake spoke again, his voice lowered, I knew he had gone to her.

"Why can't you see that that's exactly what I was doing for you? Do you really think you would have accomplished all that you have if you had stayed with me? Look at the life you've lived. The business you've built. I don't regret for one second giving up my dreams, knowing you have lived yours."

I could hear my mother crying. "You're an idiot, Jake Rimmel, if you think I've been living my dreams all this time. You weren't there. *My dream* never came true."

"You're wrong, Sophie. You can't see it, but you're wrong. You've had a better life than I ever could have given you. I am happy running my father's business. I married a woman who was happy being my wife. Staying home. Raising our children. Asking you to live that life would have been like taking one of your father's horses and locking it in a stall for all eternity. You were never meant to stay put, Sophie. You were meant to run free. And I'd be damned if I had allowed myself to tie you down and hold you back in any way."

I was listening to them so intently, I barely noticed the tears that had started running down my own cheeks. Jake didn't get it. My mother would never have been held back by him. I may never have known the wild girl she was, but I knew the force she was to be reckoned with today. My father had understood it. He hadn't loved her for it the way that Jake clearly had, but he had known that she would do whatever she set out to, regardless of whether he was coming along or not.

In that moment, I felt a surge of gratitude wash over me, knowing that Emerson and I hadn't followed in their footsteps, had stopped before we'd made the same mistake. We'd never waste years of our lives being apart because we understood, same as my mother had, that life was what you made of it. Life was about the choices you made for yourself. Not the choices made for you by others.

I had barely come to my conclusion when I felt his hand slide out of mine and in a moment of horror I realized, Emerson had sided with Jake.

The pain that seared through me as I dropped her hand from mine was enough to take my breath away. And, when I watched her head turn down to look at the break in our hold and then move up to meet my eyes, the panic in her face told me she understood.

"What are you doing?" she whispered, her words rushed with fear.

"The right thing." And it was all I could do to stare straight ahead and walk out. There would be no turning back. There would be no changing my mind.

Chapter 14

It was Steph who found me later that evening, a pile on the floor of that hallway. I hadn't been able to move other than to slide down the wall until I hit the ground where I stayed undisturbed for hours. I had been too shocked to even cry. I'd just sat there, staring at the nothingness in front of me, wondering how everything had changed so fast. How I had been so happy one moment and devastated the next.

I had no idea what had become of my mother or Jake. Somewhere in the midst of my own unraveling romance, I had lost track of theirs.

"I don't want to go back to the farm," I said quietly as she helped me to my feet.

"Then we won't. Where do you want to go? Tell me. I'll take you." I was barely standing when I flung both my arms around her neck and hugged her tight. I had come to rely on Steph so much over the last few years. She had become my rock. More solid than even Tori, whose friendship was still based on the girl I'd been in first grade.

"I just want to get out of here. I want to go home."

A few hours later and we were sitting on a plane headed back to New York. I was done with Kentucky. The Ashcrafts could have it. And Emerson with it.

I spent all of Sunday in my bed wallowing, but come Monday morning I was back at work, taking my life by the horns, so to speak. I understood everything perfectly now. My mother's rigid work ethics. Her contentedness with being alone after the divorce. She had already found her soul mate. Knew who he was. Where he was. What was the point in going out and looking for something no longer left to find. And without love, what was there? Work. That's what.

The only way to put my heart out of commission was to let my head take over. And my head was brilliant. It was full of all kinds of amazing creative design ideas and I showed up Monday morning ready to start sketching. I was finally going to stop talking about it and actually produce my own line of wedding wear.

Not surprisingly, I felt a new sort of kinship with my mother, one I was fully prepared to build upon, expecting to have someone to genuinely commiserate with. However, my hopes for shared sorrows were short lived when in a strange twist of fate, Jake showed up at the office three days after our return.

He had made an all-out fool of himself on behalf of my mother. Had announced to the entire place that he was in love with her. Had shared with everyone his memories. The first time they'd met. The last time he'd seen her. The moment he'd known he loved her. The speech had been beautiful and by the end of it my mother's real dream had finally come true. Jake was hers. He'd always been hers. Just as she'd always been his. And now, the whole world knew it.

My mother wasn't the only one suddenly living happily ever after. I knew Steph was still talking to Blake, and even though she was trying to hide it from me, I knew she was falling for him head over heels. She'd be a goner in no time, so in my spare time, which was usually around four a.m., I would find myself browsing the jobsites in search of local schools hiring for guidance counselors. I liked Blake, but I wasn't about to give Steph up without a fight.

Two weeks after Savannah's wedding and I received an email from her thanking me again for everything I'd done to help save her day. I was half-heartedly browsing through the pictures she'd sent of their honeymoon in Italy when Steph showed up in my doorway.

"Cal."

I looked up. Something was wrong. "What?"

"I just got a call from Blake. Cal…there's been an accident."

I was eerily still, moving in slow motion even while Steph's voice seemed strangely distant suddenly.

"What kind of an accident?" My hands were gripping onto the armrests of my chair without my noticing.

"Emerson. He was on his way to deliver some horses in North Carolina. He was driving through the mountains when a semi veered out of its lane and hit him."

"I have to get to the hospital."

I had no recollection of moving from my chair and across the room, but I was already running past her.

"Cal, wait." Steph reached for my arm, but I pulled it from her grasp.

"No. I'm going to the hospital. I don't care if he wants to see me or not. I have to go. I have to make sure he's okay."

"He's not at the hospital." My mother's voice cut through me like a knife.

"What do you mean? Where is he?" I could feel the hysteria building up within me.

"They haven't found him yet. Apparently the truck and trailer were pushed up against the guard rail, but it was giving out against the weight. Witnesses said they saw

Emerson get out of the truck to free the horses, but the shift of the weight and the movement…it was too much. The trailer slid and the truck went with it. And Emerson…"

I couldn't breathe. I couldn't do anything. Except run. I ran, faster than I'd ever run in my life. "I'm going to the airport. Someone book me a flight by the time I get there."

"Calista," my mother called after me, but I wasn't stopping.

"I'm going!"

By the time I arrived at the scene of the accident I couldn't have told a soul how I had traveled there. Everything had passed in a blur and the only thing that had been racing through my mind on repeat was how I needed to find Emerson because I would not live the rest of my life knowing that my chance at true love, my chance for true happiness had died by the time I was twenty-three all because he'd been too pigheaded and proud to let me love him.

I ran straight for the first policeman who crossed my path. "Have you found him yet? Is there any news?" The entire section of the highway had been blocked off while rescue workers continued to attempt to scale the steep drop off in search of Emerson.

"Ma'am, you can't be over here. You need to get back behind the tape please."

"You don't understand. The man you're looking for, he's mine. I'm not going anywhere."

His face softened and he took my elbow, gently leading me over to one of the police cars.

"You can stay. But you have to promise not to leave this car. I will send someone over here to update you on the situation momentarily, alright?"

I nodded. "Thank you."

I waited until his back was turned and then abandoned my post to see for myself where Emerson had fallen. I heard myself gasp when I peered out over the edge. The drop off was deeper than I had expected. And the mangled mess of trailer and truck gave little to hope for when I realized that they'd caught on fire at some point after the crash. Probably some sort of explosion.

"Ma'am, I thought we agreed that you would wait by the car."

"We did. I'm sorry." A thought flashed through my mind. "Was there a dog?"

The officer looked confused. "A dog?"

"Yes, a dog. I was told he released the horses before the trailer went down the mountain. Was there a dog as well when you found them?"

He shook his head. "No, ma'am. No, dog."

My heart began to pound in my chest, beating stronger with this sudden hope. I took another step closer to the edge, barely evading the officer's grasp. "REESIE. REEEEEEE-SIIEEE."

"Ma'am, I really need you to take a step back," he insisted.

"No. Listen to me. This dog goes with him everywhere. He wouldn't have freed the horses and not Reesie. If he's out there. She's with him." I turned back to shout once more, "REESIE!"

I continued calling her, even as the policeman was dragging me back to the safety of his car. I screamed louder, desperate and certain that she would show herself any moment. And then, "Reesie." There she was. Her brown coat was covered in dust and she was limping as she came slinking through what remained of the railing and trotted over to me.

"The dog. *Holy* – Guys! Over here! We've got something over here!" The officer had let go of me and was running over to where Reesie had just appeared, waving the others over for back up.

"Reesie, go get 'im. Go get Emerson. Good girl, go." I pointed back out to where she'd just come from, and she understood. Moving slowly due to her own injuries, she made her way back down to where she'd been hiding in a group of trees several hundred feet away from where the truck and trailer had wound up.

There, lying unconscious and broken between the tree trunks which had stopped his fall, was Emerson. Alive.

I burst into tears the moment I heard the rescue workers announce that he was breathing. Everything would be alright now. He would be alright. And, in turn, so would I.

The officer who'd been standing with me before came back to stay with me. "You know, you probably saved his life. I doubt we ever would have found him there on our own."

I just nodded, unable to speak.

A helicopter arrived shortly after to take Emerson to the hospital, while I chose to take a ride from the policeman. I couldn't leave Reesie. Not after everything she'd already been through. Of course, I hadn't been the only one to rush to North Carolina. Noonie Skeeter and Poppy had made the drive as soon as they'd heard about the accident. Spence had been on his way, too. A few phone calls later and they were all meeting me down at the hospital where Noonie took Reesie from me to find a vet while I found Emerson.

By some miracle, Emerson had escaped the near death experience with minor injuries all things considered. He'd hit his head pretty badly, and broken several ribs and suffered some internal bleeding from the blunt force trauma which had required immediate surgery, but aside from that it was mostly all just bumps and bruises. And Spence had assured me over and over again that he would be fine.

It was well after midnight and I was sitting in his room beside his bed, waiting for him to wake up. The nurse had warned me that it could take a while, but I didn't care. I sat there, silently holding his hand, waiting for that last bit of relief I would feel when he finally opened his eyes again.

"Liss?" His voice was raspy and raw from being intubated. Still semi-unconscious, he squeezed my hand softly.

"I'm right here." I whispered. "I'm beyond pissed at you by the way."

His lips curled up ever so slightly. "Alright, Firecracker."

"And hey, next time you want to see me, just give me a call. This whole 'throw yourself down the side of a mountain' thing tad dramatic, no?"

"Worked though, didn't it?" His eyes still hadn't opened, but I didn't care. It was enough to hear his voice again. Better even actually.

He fell asleep again and I spent the rest of the night sitting beside him, perfectly contented.

When I woke up again I was surprised to see it was daytime. I had no idea how long I'd been sleeping except that Lissy was still sitting in the chair beside me, her head resting on the side of my mattress. I couldn't remember much of anything, but I had a vague memory of talking to her at some point during the night.

The closer I looked at her the more I realized how disheveled her appearance was. Her feet were bare and her clothes were covered in dirt and dust. Had she been in the accident with me? No. Absolutely not. I hadn't seen her since the wedding. I had made sure of it. And yet, here she was.

Her head stirred and slowly lifted.

"You're awake." There was something in her eyes I hadn't seen there before. I didn't like it. And I had a feeling I'd put it there.

"How long have you been sitting here?"

She shrugged. "I don't know. How long you been laying there?"

"Liss, you shouldn't be here. Go home."

I had expected her to get upset. To have her feelings hurt. To storm out. But she laughed.

"Don't even start with me, asshole. I'm not going anywhere. And you can't do a damn thing about it because you're on bed rest."

I hadn't expected that.

"Did you just call me an asshole?"

"Did you just act like one? You almost died, Emerson. You fell down a freaking mountain. I saved your life, by the way. Just ask Officer Grayson, he'll tell you all about it. I'm like your own personal Wonder Woman now. So, you're like, indebted to me. I have *big* plans to collect, my friend."

I chuckled and it sent a pain through my side. "Shit. Don't make me laugh, Liss."

"Then don't make me cry." Her face had turned serious in the blink of an eye.

"I never meant to make you cry. You have to know that." Now I was about to lose it. Walking away from Lissy had been the hardest damn thing I'd ever done in my life. And I knew, I fucking knew, there was no way I'd be able to do it a second time.

"I do know. That's why I'm going to forgive you. This time. Thing is, Emerson, we don't choose our soul mates. We don't choose who they are or when they show up in our lives. We don't choose the circumstances or the setting. It just happens. The only choice we have is whether we acknowledge it or not, and if it's worth the fight." She was looking down at her own hands. "Noonie Skeeter told me that a while back and I didn't really understand it. Then, when it finally made sense to me, I thought maybe *you* didn't understand it. But now, now I get it. I really get it. We both acknowledged it. And we both decided it was worth the fight. Only problem is, we have very different ways of fighting. You, selfless hero slash martyr that you are, would risk falling off of a mountain to set those you love free. While I, hopeless romantic as it turns out *I am*, will stand on the edge of that mountain and wait against all odds, even when there are no signs indicating that you will ever return."

She lifted her gaze, tears in her eyes, but a smile forging its way through all of the hurt. "In any event, your way will result in one of two ways. One, you stay down there, buried in the rubble on the side of that mountain. You die and we both lose. Or, two, which I find more favorable, you climb your way back up to the top where I'm still

193

waiting. I win, but *you* still lose." She was leaning in over me, getting closer to my face, her lips lingering near mine in a way that made it hard for me to think.

"So, the way I figure, if you're going to lose either way you might as well just *let me win*." And she was kissing me. Softly at first, until I reached up and pressed her to me hard. Taking her with my mouth, wrapping those long strands of soft silky hair around my hands and easing the ache that had ripped at me ever since I'd held her last. How had I ever thought that I could live without this? That I could live without her? Liss was right. My way had me losing either way. It was time to let her win.

Chapter 15

Six months after the accident and my world was never the same. Starting with my mother, who hadn't waited long to announce she and Jake Rimmel had finally eloped. By some strange turn of events, Poppy had been the first to congratulate them. Personally, I think Noonie Skeeter had made him do it, but either way, the path had been cleared for Emerson and me. Which made things that much easier for him to move forward in taking over Burke's position, once he was able to come back to work. A promotion he was given in spite of Burke's warning to the contrary.

In the meantime, my mother and I had decided it was time for Luvalle Weddings to branch out. Jack found himself suddenly bumped up into a position of power which he gladly embraced as the new head of the Manhattan office, while Steph opted to come along on our new adventure and open the new Lexington Location with us. I told myself that it was because of all my awesomeness, but even I knew I was lying to myself. It didn't have shit to do with me. It was all about the Blake.

My plans for creating my own line were still moving full steam ahead and I was loving the theme. It had a whole country meets fairy tale vibe happening. I blamed Savannah for this. She was more than happy to take the credit, while Tori had accepted the move to Kentucky on the one condition that she would get first choice once the collection was finished.

Even though our new shop was coming along splendidly and came fully equipped with a design study for me to work in, I was finding that all of my best creations were happening out at Ashcraft farms, usually sitting up on some stack of hay bales or an overturned wheel barrow where I could easily glance up and see Emerson working with the horses and doing what he did best.

Today, I had set up shop on a barrel filled with alfalfa cubes. Jake had delivered a whole load of them just that morning and I had found a stray still out in the aisle waiting to be moved into the feed room. It had been perfectly located in the entrance of the barn, providing an excellent view, as well as a perfect combination of light for work and shade for staying cool. Naturally, I had climbed right up, crossed my legs Indian style and started sketching away on my notepad.

I was so engulfed in the dress I was working on, I didn't even see Emerson walking up.

"Hey. Staring contest. Go."

I smiled, locking eyes with him. "You know, I'm much better at these now than I was back then."

"Oh yeah?" He took a step closer, maintaining his stare.

"Definitely. You're going down mister." Without breaking my gaze, I reached up to grab a handful of his shirt and tugged him in toward me. Then, when he was close enough, I playfully flicked my tongue over his soft lips. He was a goner. His eyes closed as he sunk into my lips, kissing me deeply and wrapping both arms around me.

When he broke away several long minutes later, he grinned sheepishly.

"I win," I teased still holding him close by his shirt.

"I guess that means you get a prize."

I watched as he reached into his back pocket and pulled out a card.

"What's this?" My fingers trembled as I touched the envelope. This scene had played out once before between us. Only the roles had been reversed. Surely that wasn't by coincidence.

Slowly, I slid my finger under the flap of the envelope and flipped it open. A single paged card was inside. The letters SAVE THE DATE boldly on display before I even took it out. I swallowed hard and carefully retrieved the card. It was the one I'd given him over seventeen years ago.

"You kept it? All this time?"

"I wasn't supposed to forget." He reached over and took my hand, the one holding the card. Then, he gently turned it over. My eyes went wide at the sight. There was ring taped to the back of it.

Speechless, I watched as Emerson removed it.

"Seems that knowing the Ashcraft family has been shaping my life in different ways for as long as I can remember, Liss. They saved me from being homeless as a child. They gave me a best friend who's been like a brother to me. Then, when I grew up to be a man, they led me to my passion, the thing I'll do for the rest of my life. For a long time I was certain nothing else could ever trump those gifts that they'd given me. Except, as it turns out, something else already had. Years ago, at the lake house."

He slid the ring onto my finger and held it tight in place. "Feels like I've damn near lost you about a hundred times already, Liss. What do you say, we put a stop to that pattern?"

"Emerson Barrett, are you asking me to save the date...of our wedding?"

"I am. Calista Luvalle, will you marry me?"

Like there was ever any question.

Epilogue

Exactly nineteen years after I'd drawn up my first wedding dress, I was actually wearing one. The top was an ivory strapless sweetheart neckline made completely out of lace and paired with a full length, tiered a-line skirt. It had a delicate beaded belt at the waist and was completed with a chapel train. It was also entirely inspired by the crayon colored design I'd found stuffed away in my old scrapbook from that fateful summer at the lake house.

"You know, I think that may be the most beautiful gown you've ever designed." Steph was standing behind me, cinching up the corset. "You going to add it to the fall collection?"

It'd be the second year since I started selling my own collection. In that short time, a handful of high-end boutiques had already picked up several of the designs and I had even shown at Bridal Fashion week in the previous spring. Something I mentioned to Poppy more than once, just in case he had any lingering doubts about my relationship with Emerson and whether it was holding me back in any way.

I stepped out in front of the mirror to get another look at the dress. Not that I hadn't paraded around in it plenty already. There had been several days when I had left it on from morning until night, just because I could and it was so freaking pretty.

"It would go nicely with the rest of the dresses we have picked out for the line." I held up the skirt in each hand and gently swayed back in forth letting the tulle make that swishing sound I liked so much. "Speaking of pretty dresses. When am I going to get to make one for you?"

"When I have a need for one," she said, slyly avoiding my gaze.

"What, you two can't set a date?"

Steph looked up abruptly, then studied my face for a moment, probably trying to determine if I knew. And I did. She and Blake had gone away on a long weekend getaway to Cancun just last month. When she returned to work the following Tuesday I couldn't help but notice she had a rather unusual tan line on one of her fingers. And since the ring was absent but Blake wasn't, I concluded she was waiting until after my wedding to tell me about it. Afraid to steal my bridal thunder or something. Meanwhile, I hadn't wanted to deny her the moment of making the grand announcement. Until now apparently, since the words had just sort of slipped right out.

"How long have you known?"

"When did you get back from Cancun?" I laughed. "Seriously Steph. People flash me their ring fingers on a daily basis. I'm like programmed now. Forget making eye contact with people. I'm looking at their hands. And you can't go around rocking a ring tan line and think it will go unnoticed."

She grinned sheepishly. "So, you want to see it?"

"Obviously!" I went and huddled beside her as she retrieved a sparkling ring from her purse and slid it onto her finger. "Ooh, it's gorgeous."

"I know!" Steph giggled and it was almost the girly kind. Apparently being extra giddy could bring that out in all of us.

"So, back to your dress."

She glanced over at the fluff of white shrouding my entire body. "We'll talk after you get back from your honeymoon. That will give us plenty of time to get all the details worked out before winter."

"The lake house will look amazing all covered in snow." I winked at her as I made my way back to the mirror for one last glance. If we kept it up, this place would be better known for its weddings than the family reunions.

There was a knock on the door and my mother walked in with Tori in tow.

"What is the hold up in here? I've got an antsy groom standing out on a dock thinking about jumping if you don't show up to marry him soon."

Tori squeezed past her into the room. "No worries. I've got Spence and Blake blocking the water. In the meantime, look at you!"

I twirled around bringing to life my inner six year old. "Not bad for someone you thought was never getting married, huh?"

She dismissed it with a wave. "What did I know? Besides. If I had known there was an Emerson out here waiting for you, I never would have bothered with the Tylers, the Jasons or the Prestons of Manhattan. It's clear to me now why none of them ever stuck." She gasped. "You know Hallmark should totally make a movie about you two."

I reached out and hugged her close. "Yeah. I'm pretty sure they already did that. A few times."

With my mother rushing everyone along, we finally made our way downstairs and out back to the water where everyone else was already gathered.

The wedding was small. Only Poppy and Noonie Skeeter were in attendance in addition to Jake, my mother's date. My father had of course been invited, but seen to it to politely decline due to a conflict in his schedule. I had expected as much and had finally reached a place in my life where I was actually relieved to know that he wouldn't be there. He'd been so removed from my life for so long, it would have taken away from the intimate experience to have a stranger in our midst. Sounds sad, but it was true, and more importantly, I felt content with it.

With Tori and Steph leading the way, my mother took my hand, and together we made the long walk down to the end of the dock. The same place my relationship with Emerson had first been cemented a million years ago with nothing more than a bit of faith and a fishing pole.

Standing there in his classic black tux, with his hands nervously swaying at his sides and a smile from ear to ear, I knew I was marrying the most handsome man I'd ever meet. And while part of me had worried that making this walk down the aisle would scare me, that the enormity of the gesture and the unyielding power of the promise I was meant to make to him would have me itching to escape, I had never felt more at ease. More confident.

All the things I'd always thought I feared the most, were floating off into oblivion as I walked along the dock to the boy who had always held my hand and now would *always* hold my heart.

Ten Years Later

"Mama? Who is this?" Emmalyn was holding the picture frame in her sweet chubby little hands looking down at it with her tiny brows fixed in a confused scrunch.

"You can't tell?" I tapped the glass slightly with my fingertip. "That's me and Daddy."

She gazed up at me. "It is?"

I nodded. "Absolutely." I took the frame from her and led her over to the kitchen table where I had a glass of milk and a plate of cookies already waiting for us. "Did I ever tell you that Mommy and Daddy met right here, at the lake house?"

Her eyes grew wide. "No."

"We sure did." I smiled.

"Mama, how did you know that you wanted to marry Daddy?"

I laughed, thinking about little Michael Hatcher and how much Emmalyn had followed him around last week when Blake and Steph had joined us here.

"Well, thing is, baby, until I was six, I was fairly certain I would grow up to marry Prince Eric from The Little Mermaid. Then came the first summer that your Ne-ma Sophie brought me out here to the family lake house which was when I first met Daddy. After that, Prince Eric was history."

The end.

Author K.S. Thomas

Dog Lover who likes her pastries full of cream and sugar….oh…and I write some ☺

Aside from being an author, I am also a mom to a beautiful little girl. I tell everyone I named her after my great-grandmother (because that's the mature answer), but really, I named her after my favorite princess – just so happens I got lucky and they had the same name…If I wasn't a writer, I would work on a horse ranch – I'm an animal lover (in addition to dogs, horses are at the top of my list). I wear flip-flops pretty much everywhere I go. I would rather stay awake until 5 am than get up at 5 am (years of bar tending have left their mark), if I can, I'm going to the beach AND I will always be nice to people who bring me chocolate…or coffee…if you bring me both, I'll probably love you forever.

A gypsy at heart, I write the way I live, following the story wherever it may lead, always ready to start the next one. This is clearly reflected in my body of work which to date includes everything from Children's Lit to Thrillers.

I happily reside in sunny Florida (for now) and can be contacted via my blog (www.friedgatortail.com), my website (www.ksthomas.net) or the following social media sites ~

Facebook: www.facebook.com/friedgatortail
Twitter: @friedgatortail
Goodreads: www.goodreads.com/friedgatortail
Pinterest: www.pinterest.com/friedgatortail

Books by K.S. Thomas include ~

I Call Him Brady
Salty
Country Girls
Blood Bound
Drive
This Christmas
Lucky In Love
Getting Lucky (A Lucky Novella)
The Final Descendants And The Well Of Wishes Lost
(Book One)

Upcoming Releases For 2014

Lost Avalon

Fame, fortune and a future paved with rock and roll gold. Blaise Nolan has it all. With his brooding good looks, haunting voice and troubled lyrics of a soul gone lost, it's no wonder Finding Nolan has been climbing the music charts with back to back hits. Only Blaise didn't wind up brooding, haunted and lost by accident...

Avalon Jennison has been the girl next door since she was five. The best friend since she was eight. The band manager since she was sixteen and the keeper of his secrets always. Ava's been there every step of the way, helping him live his dreams and keeping his nightmares at bay. But the years of putting Blaise's needs above her own are about to be over.

Everyone is about to find out what she has always known: There's no Finding Nolan without Avalon.

Unhurt

Joss Kelley's life has never been easy, but these days she's quite confident when it comes to rolling with the punches. No matter who's throwing them. So when her son's father shows up out of the blue threatening to take him, Joss stops at nothing to sway the judge in her favor. Even if it means making impromptu marriage proposals to random strangers she finds sitting in her brother's bar.

After 9/11 Derek Tice knew exactly what he wanted to do with his life. Until six months ago when he was honorably discharged after spending thirteen years as a Navy Seal. Now, with no more operations to plan or missions to complete, he's feeling strangely lost and useless. Since going back is not an option, he has no choice but to find a new worthy cause he can dedicate his life to.

Joss Kelley and her son just might be it.

Printed in Great Britain
by Amazon